Arthur Schnitzler (1862–1931) was born and died in Vienna. He was raised in a middle-class family, his father being a prominent throat specialist among whose patients were many of the leading actors and singers of his time. Schnitzler attended the exclusive Academisches Gymnasium and began writing when a young boy, but seemed set to follow his father into medicine, qualifying as a doctor in 1885. He was very interested in psychiatry and experimented with hypnosis, and some scholars believed that he anticipated some of Freud's ideas. In 1903 he married the actress Olga Gussman, with whom he had two children.

Schnitzler's writings challenged contemporary bourgeois morality, and as a result of this he endured a great deal of personal abuse. His work suffered under the Nazi regime, but since the sixties interest in it has revived. He wrote some twenty-three full length and ten one-act plays, and many prose works.

Shaun Whiteside was educated at the Royal School, Dungannon, and King's College, Cambridge, where he graduated with a First in Modern Languages. He has translated widely from French, German and Italian. His translation of Nietzsche's *Birth of Tragedy* is published in Penguin Classics.

Martin Swales was educated at the Universities of Cambridge and Birmingham, and he is currently Professor of German at University College London. He has published studies of Arthur Schnitzler, the German Novelle, the German Bildungsroman, Thomas Mann, and German Realism.

Beatrice and Her Son

ARTHUR SCHNITZLER

Translated by Shaun Whiteside
Introduction by Martin Swales

PENGUIN BOOKS

PENGUIN BOOKS

Published by the Penguin Group
Penguin Books Ltd, 27 Wrights Lane, London w8 5tz, England
Penguin Putnam Inc., 375 Hudson Street, New York, New York 10014, USA
Penguin Books Australia Ltd, Ringwood, Victoria, Australia
Penguin Books Canada Ltd, 10 Alcorn Avenue, Toronto, Ontario, Canada M4V 3B2
Penguin Books (NZ) Ltd, Private Bag 102902, NSMC, Auckland, New
Zealand

Penguin Books Ltd, Registered Offices: Harmondsworth, Middlesex, England

First published in German as *Frau Beate und ihr Sohn* in 1913
Published in Penguin Books 1999
10 9 8 7 6 5 4 3 2 1

Translation copyright © Shaun Whiteside, 1999
Introduction copyright © Martin Swales, 1999

Set in 10.75/13.75 pt Monotype Sabon
Typeset by Rowland Phototypesetting Ltd, Bury St Edmunds, Suffolk
Printed in England by Clays Ltd, St Ives plc

Introduction

Arthur Schnitzler lived from 1862 to 1931. In terms both of his actual and of his fictional experiential world, he is inseparable from one city: Vienna, from its outward and inward topography, from its materiality and its mentality. He came from the prosperous upper bourgeoisie. His father was a celebrated throat specialist, and was frequently consulted by the leading actors and singers of the day. The son seemed destined for a career in medicine. He completed his training very successfully at Vienna University, writing his doctorate on the role of hypnosis in dealing with cases of acute loss of voice. It seemed that the course of his life lay open and unproblematic before him. But increasingly he became drawn to imaginative literature. And once it was obvious that a viable career as a professional writer beckoned, he abandoned medicine (the private practice, on which he had embarked in 1893, was at best a half-hearted enterprise). In the course of his literary career, he wrote both prose (two novels, but the bulk of his narrative output is in the shorter mode) and drama (both full-length and one-act plays).

Outwardly his life was secure – and, in its sophisticated pleasures and irresolute erotic attachments, not dissimilar from that of most of his class and gender at the time. But there were also profound disturbances, and he felt them acutely. One was the emergence in Vienna, from the early years of the twentieth century, of a virulent form of anti-Semitism, personified most unsettlingly in the charming but malign figure of Vienna's charismatic mayor Karl Lueger. In the autobiographical account of his early years, *Youth in Vienna*, Schnitzler makes the following comment on Lueger: 'There were and are people who saw it as a redeeming feature that, even in his most virulent anti-Semitic phase, he retained a personal affection for many Jews – and made no secret of it. To me that always seemed the strongest proof of his moral dubiousness.'

Schnitzler, like so many of his generation, class and profession, was a Jew who was thoroughly assimilated into Austrian society. The shock of being told that he did not, after all, belong was profound. Yet he felt unable to espouse the solution offered by a fellow inhabitant of Vienna, Theodor Herzl, whose book *The Jewish State* is the founding tract of Zionism. Schnitzler could not share in such once-and-for-all enthusiasms; he was, quite simply, too much of a sceptic. But the hurt caused by the rising tide of anti-Semitism went deep (witness his novel *The Road into the Open* and the drama *Professor Bernhardi*).

The other great upheaval was the First World War, which finally dismembered the great straggling and struggling relic of Habsburg dynastic rule, the Austro-Hungarian Empire. Schnitzler had no time for the bellicose enthusiasms of 1914; once again he was a sceptical, and anguished, onlooker. The despair was great. He lived for almost twenty years beyond the outbreak of hostilities. But, fascinatingly, in his creative work, he never got to, still less beyond, the cataclysm. Even the works written after 1914 are set before 1914. Many commentators have registered this fact as bespeaking a damaging limitation of his vision. Yet it has to be remembered that the period before 1914 was peculiarly, one might even say seismically, endowed with intimations of cultural disturbance – and was (and is) on that account of surpassing interest. Schnitzler, like so many of the gifted minds of his generation, felt the tremors before they struck. And the resultant questioning became the defining signature of European modernity. The list of great names who first emerged to prominence in the pre-1914 years is awe-inspiring: in music, Mahler, Schoenberg, Berg, Webern; in the visual arts, Klimt and Schiele; in psychology, Sigmund Freud; in literature, Hofmannsthal, Rilke, Kafka, Musil – and Schnitzler. In their different ways all these figures register a shifting of the ground of their culture; and this generates a sense of subliminal, subtextual disquiet. The subtext was felt with particular urgency because the foreground social text of the time was characterized by a kind of self-congratulatory immobility, an omnipresent paralysis of both the individual will and the body politic. Stefan Grossmann, a contemporary of Schnitzler, comments: 'I had in the last years before the war in Vienna the feeling of standing in a locked room, which had not been aired for months, with dusty windows that were rusted shut.' It was precisely this strangely becalmed condition that gave the spokesmen of the modern world a ferocious sense of swirling, ungovernable subtexts – and it also served Lueger's demagogic purposes well. He was, of course, not the only one. Adolf Hitler cut his political teeth in Vienna.

Schnitzler registers the subliminal disturbances of pre-1914 Austrian culture in a number of characteristic ways. One is – and this distinguishes him from the majority of his great literary contemporaries – he retains a thoroughgoing sense of literary realism, a sense that, to put it most simply, he is writing of one time and of one place. Invariably his characters radiate an identity that goes with social class, profession, domicile in Vienna, and so on. (One thinks particularly of *Lieutenant Gustl*, which is a masterly portrait of the ebb and flow of mendacious and aggressive impulses that fill the mind of a young Austrian army officer.) Another is – and this is a common factor of the literary production of the time – he has the highly developed ability to move close to, even to be artistically complicit in, the intense but anchorless inner lives of the characters. Time and time again he explores them at a moment of crisis in their lives; but the crisis may prove not so much cathartic as disorientating. As a narrator, Schnitzler is incomparable in his ability to eavesdrop on the mind under stress; he is a master of free indirect speech and interior monologue. In this context it is pertinent to recall that Freudian psychoanalysis is supremely a verbal therapy. To say this is to touch on subterranean connections, but not to equate, Schnitzler's narrative art with Freud's project. The two men, in fact, had surprisingly little contact with each other; in a famous letter to Schnitzler Freud invokes the similarity of their views on the role of the subconscious mind, on the polarity of love and death – but this common ground produced in Freud a need to avoid his great literary compatriot 'from a kind of unease at meeting my double', as he put it. In any event, Schnitzler was weightily concerned to understand the particular, socially specific parameters of the psyche of his characters, whereas Freud's model of the psyche is timeless and essentializing. Once again, to reiterate an argument that has already been put, Schnitzler was modest and sceptical in the claims that he made. The third feature of his writing that deserves mention is his diagnostic acuity. Not for nothing was he trained as a doctor. He once remarked in an aphorism that whoever had been a doctor could never cease to be one, because medicine was a whole way of viewing the world. For the most part, Schnitzler is a very unjudgemental writer. Even so, for all his detailed stenography of the swirling inner life, he retains a vital intimation of ironic, socially and morally critical, distance, an astringency of vision that knows of the delusions and desperate self-deceptions of the characters. At his finest, Schnitzler holds the world that he knows so well at bay, at one (artistic) remove. Perhaps his art offered the better, more scrupulous, more tactful, at once more compassionate and more critical possibility of diagnosis of his age and culture than did medicine.

Beatrice and Her Son appeared in 1913. It focuses on a particular crisis in the life of Beatrice Heinold, whose husband, a famous actor, died suddenly some five years before the story opens. Beatrice is on holiday with her son, Hugo. The story begins with an acute intimation of disturbance and transition; Beatrice watches her son sleeping and registers the disquiet and pain that play across his face. She has sensed from a number of tiny incidents recently that the innocence of childhood has been displaced in Hugo by the onset of puberty. And, as the subsequent course of the story makes clear, that unruly, foreign dimension of desire is by no means confined to the adolescents, to Hugo and his friends Fritz and Rudi; rather, it is balefully omnipresent in the society as a whole. We register it in virtually all the acquaintances with whom Beatrice comes into contact. She is still an attractive woman; and this is acknowledged by all those (and particularly by the men) she meets – with greater or lesser degrees of sympathy, interest, resentment, jealousy. The manifestation of desire is often sudden and violent. At one point, in the prosperous villa of the Welponers, Beatrice watches four young people playing tennis. She delights in their physical beauty and movement. Yet as soon as they have stopped playing, the atmosphere changes and sultry currents of sexual tension come to the fore:

> strangely, almost painfully, Beatrice felt the atmosphere, so pure before, growing steamy and forming storm clouds, and it made her think: how would this evening end if all of a sudden, through some miracle, all the rules of morality were abolished from the world, and these young people were able to follow unhindered their secret urges, of which perhaps even they were unaware? And suddenly it occurred to her that such lawless worlds did exist; that she herself had risen from just such a world, and still bore its scent in her hair.

In the precariously sustained equanimity of her widowhood, Beatrice is distressed to register such disturbances. But that unruly world is not only around her; it is also within her. When Fritz, a schoolfriend of Hugo, makes advances to her, she offers little resistance. Ironically, in the opening sequence of the story she goes to see Fortunata, an older woman, an erstwhile actress, because she fears that Hugo may be starting an affair with her. She extracts a promise from Fortunata that nothing of that sort will be allowed to occur. But later in the story such a thing does occur – and it is Beatrice who is the older woman in the affair. The patterning of Schnitzler's story, whereby Beatrice gets drawn into what she initially repudiates, is implacable. For example: when she notices that Fortunata is naked under her linen dress, this serves to confirm the aggression and resentment within her; she disapproves of the sluttishness of the woman with whom she is talking:

> At the same time she noticed that Fortunata's feet were
> bare in their sandals, and that she was naked beneath her
> white linen dress.

But later in the story Beatrice rejoices that she provokes
desire, even though she despises the figure who feels that
desire:

> And again she looked quickly at the bank director, now
> walking silently along by her side, but she was almost
> frightened to feel around her lips a smile that had come
> from the depths of her soul and which said undeniably,
> almost shamelessly, more clearly than any words could
> have done: I know you desire me, and I am pleased.

And later still, just before the first night of love with Fritz,
she feels, with a tremor of sexual pleasure, the outlines
of her own body beneath her clothes:

> Why strange? She was as young as, perhaps younger than,
> that Fortunata. And all of a sudden, with agonizing clarity
> and yet with painful pleasure, she could feel the outlines
> of her body beneath her thin clothing.

In such moments of precise structural articulation
Schnitzler holds in critical focus the swirling flux of Beatrice's inner life.

In the course of the story Beatrice moves from being
a blameless widow and concerned mother to a figure
submerged in immense sexual turmoil. Once her respectable, orderly life begins to unravel, not only the present
but also the past becomes sucked into the vortex. Her
memories of her husband modulate from images of the
unforgettable partner who offered her the fusion of bourgeois respectability (as husband) on the one hand and
pure sexual adventurer (as actor) on the other to a convic-
tion that he was consistently and systematically unfaithful

to her. As soon as that becomes a possible version of Beatrice's cherished past, then nothing, no selfhood, no relationship, no experience is proof against the erosion:

> Where am I? She stretched her hands skywards. How much deeper will you let me sink! Is there no resting place? What is it that makes me so wretched, so pitiful? What makes me clutch at random into the void, making me no better than Fortunata and all the women of that kind? And suddenly, her heartbeat failing, she knew what was making her miserable: the ground on which she had walked in safety for years was rocking, and the sky above her was darkening: the only man she had loved, her Ferdinand, had been a liar.

That ineluctable transformation of Beatrice's experience from coherence into anarchy culminates in the final scene of the story. Beatrice senses the despair in Hugo; she pleads with him to confide in her because – as she puts it in one of the darkest ironies in Schnitzler's tale – she is a woman, a relatively young woman, who is still in touch with emotions, with the desires that burn and transfigure. She will understand:

> I'm your mother, Hugo, and I'm a woman. Bear that in mind, I'm a woman as well. You mustn't fear that you could hurt me, that you could wound my tender feelings. I've been through a lot recently. I'm not yet an . . . old woman. I understand everything. Too much, my son. You mustn't think that we are so far apart, Hugo, and that there are things you mustn't say to me.

Behind this speech there is, of course, a monstrous double meaning (one that Beatrice herself only imperfectly understands): she can reach out to Hugo precisely because she has a lover of her son's age. Hugo cuts through her mother's fine words of compassion to that other – literal – meaning when he reveals that he knows what has happened between his mother and Fritz. The story moves to an eerie climax, a kind of Wagnerian love-death in which the ecstatic coming together of mother and son, two figures who have been estranged of late, is both literally and metaphorically a primal drama. Desire is acknowledged across the gap of generation and taboo; the mother who has taken her son's best friend for her lover has, by that token, vicariously converted the son into the lover. Desire elides distinctions, makes equivalences. The bond between mother and son could not be closer – or more cankered.

On this note of searing ambiguity – and high emotion – Schnitzler's story closes. It is a remarkable tale. At one level it is, as we have seen, a family drama of mother and son. That particular drama is enacted at one particular, and untranslatable level in the German. The original title of the story is *Frau Beate und ihr Sohn*; and the specific mode of naming the main character draws attention to the shift of names, of forms of address, in the drama of relatedness. When Fritz and Beate first meet at the railway station, she calls him not Fritz but 'Herr Weber' – which acknowledges his adult status. He protests – but to no avail, although later precisely his newly acknowledged adulthood will be the source of intimacy. (It is a young man who seduces Beatrice, and not her son's schoolfriend.) When he declares his love for her, his terms of address modulate from '*gnädige Frau*' via 'Frau Beate' to 'Beate'. Even the elaborate civilities of the German language, then, become enmeshed in the flux of desire.

The family drama is, as we have seen, at the heart of Schnitzler's narrative. But there is a remark in the tale that alerts us to a number of wider implications. At one point Beatrice reflects on the libidinal madness that is everywhere in evidence – particularly as it affects the women:

> How did she live all those years since Ferdinand went away? Modest as a young girl, free of desire. Only this summer has it come upon her. Might there be something in the air this year? The women all look different; so do the girls, they have brighter, more insolent eyes, and their gestures are careless, enticing and seductive. You hear all sorts of things!

One asks oneself what might be special about this year. The answer, of course, is 'nothing' . . . except that the story appears in 1913, just at the threshold of the European catastrophe. Not, of course, that the tale is by that token to be interpreted as an allegory of Austria or Europe just before the eruption of violence. But the implications resonate unmistakably. One is very much reminded of an almost exactly contemporary work, Thomas Mann's *Death in Venice*, which was published in 1912. There too a person of blameless and orderly character leaves hold of his familiar world and goes on holiday. And there he becomes infatuated with a young person, succumbs inwardly to depravity and chaotic feeling, and finally is destroyed by the tumult he has unleashed. Some of these implications can be heard in Schnitzler's tale. It is, of course, a wonderfully observed narrative – psychologically, socially, culturally. But behind that detailed foreground we sense an unmistakably acerbic, diagnostic level of statement, one which seeks to comprehend the processes by which the surrender to intense, putatively authentic experience can ultimately prove catastrophic. And perhaps it is not too fanciful to suggest that in that diagnosis we glimpse the nemesis awaiting a whole generation, a whole culture.

Martin Swales

Beatrice and Her Son

Chapter One

She thought she had heard a sound coming from the next room. She looked up from the letter she had just begun writing, rose to her feet, took a few quiet steps to the door that stood slightly ajar, and at first glanced through the crack into the adjacent room, where her son seemed to be sleeping peacefully on the divan with the shutters closed. Only then did she step closer to him, and now she was able to watch Hugo's chest rising and falling evenly with his young boy's breath. His white, rather crumpled shirt collar was open over his throat, but otherwise Hugo was fully dressed; even his feet were clad in the hobnailed boots that he used to wear in the countryside. Clearly he had intended to lie down for only a short while in the sultry heat of the afternoon, in order, as the open textbooks and notebooks testified, to return to his studies very soon. Now he tossed his head sideways as if about to wake up; but he just stretched a few times and went on sleeping. But his mother's eyes, which had by now grown accustomed to the dusk of the room, could no longer ignore the fact that the strange tension, as though painfully taut, around the seventeen-year-old's lips, which had struck her time and again over the past few days, refused to leave the sleeping boy's face. With a sigh, Beatrice shook her head and returned to her room, closed the door quietly behind her and looked down at the letter she had just begun, which she no longer felt inclined to continue. Dr Teichmann, to whom it was addressed, was not the man to whom she could talk openly; she, who already regretted that excessively friendly smile with which she had said goodbye to him from the window of the coach before setting off. During these summer weeks in the country, memories of her husband, who had departed this life five years before, reawakened in her with especial vividness; so, internally, she particularly spurned the lawyer's advances, as yet unspoken but doubtless to be expected; and she told herself that she should not discuss her worries about Hugo with the one person who would take such a gesture less as proof of her trust than as a deliberate sign of encouragement. So she tore up the letter she had begun and walked irresolutely to the window.

The lines of the mountains on the opposite bank blurred in tremulous circles of air. From the lake below the image of the sun glittered up at her in a thousand fragments, and she eased her blinded eyes with a fleeting glance over the meadow banks, the dusty country road, the gleaming roofs of the villas and a motionless field of corn and into the green of her garden. She let her eyes and thoughts rest on the white bench below the window. She thought of how often her husband had sat there, brooding over a role – or fallen asleep, particularly when the air lay over the landscape with the sluggishness of summer, as it did again today. Then Beatrice had bent over the balcony and stroked his grey and black curls with her gentle fingers and twined them around until Ferdinand, who had soon woken up, but at first tolerated the caress while pretending to stay asleep, slowly turned and looked up at her with his bright child's eyes, which, on far-off and unforgettable

fairy-tale evenings, could look heroic and heavy as death.
But she didn't want to, she couldn't let herself think about
that; certainly not with the sighs that now involuntarily
passed her lips. For Ferdinand himself – in days long past
he had made her swear to it – wished his memory to be
consecrated cheerfully, by the carefree acceptance of fresh
happiness. And Beatrice thought: isn't it terrifying the way
we can talk of the most terrible events when everything is
flourishing, joking and easy, as if only other people were
threatened by such things, as if they couldn't happen to
us! And then it happens, and you can't understand it, yet
you take it in anyway; and time goes on, and you live;
you sleep in the same bed that you once shared with your
beloved, you drink from the same glass that he touched
with his lips, beneath the shade of the same fir trees you
pick strawberries where once you gathered them with
someone who will never go strawberry-picking again; and
you haven't ever quite understood life or death.

She had sometimes sat outside on this bench by Ferdinand's side, while the boy, embraced and followed by
his parents' tender gaze, had gone charging through the
garden with his ball or hoop. And although she knew
with her conscious mind that Hugo, who was sleeping in
there in the adjoining room, with that new painful tension
around his lips, was the same child that had played in the
garden only a few years before, she couldn't grasp it
emotionally, any more than she could the fact that Ferdinand was dead, more truly dead than Hamlet, than
Cyrano, than King Richard, in whose masks she had so
often seen him die. But perhaps this remained incomprehensible to her for ever only because no weeks of suffering
and fear had intervened between such flourishing life and
such dark death. One day Ferdinand had left home healthy

and at ease to go to some guest engagement, and an hour later he had been brought home a corpse from the railway station in whose hall he had been struck down.

While Beatrice pursued these memories, she kept feeling that something else, tormenting her like a ghost and waiting for a kind of redemption, was moving back and forth in her soul. Only after some contemplation did she become aware that the last sentence she had started in her unfinished letter, in which she wanted to write about Hugo, was giving her no peace, and that she had to steel herself to think it through to its conclusion. She was well aware that something in Hugo was either preparing itself or reaching its conclusion, something that she had expected for a long time, and which she had never considered possible. In earlier years, when he was still a child, she had cherished the idea that later she would not only be his mother but also his friend and confidante; and, until recently, when he had come to her to confess both his little misdemeanours at school and his first boyish infatuations, she had allowed herself to imagine that such a rare maternal joy was to be reserved for her. Had he not allowed her to read the touching and childish verses that he had dedicated to little Elise Weber, the sister of a fellow pupil, which the girl herself had never got to see? And only last winter, had he not admitted to his mother that a little lady, whose name he gallantly kept to himself, had kissed him on the cheek at dance class during a waltz? And last spring, had he not, almost driven to distraction, told her of two boys in his class who had spent an evening in the Prater in questionable company, and boasted that they had not come home until three o'clock in the morning? So Beatrice had dared hope that Hugo would also choose her as his confidante for more serious sensations and

experiences, and that she would be able, with encouragement and advice, to keep him from many of the sorrows
and dangers of the adolescent years. But now it turned out
that these had been merely the dreams of a spoilt mother's
heart; because when the first emotional torment came
upon him, Hugo grew alien and closed, and his mother
stood shy and helpless before a creature so new to her.

She gave a start. For in the first breath of wind of late
afternoon, like a mocking confirmation of her emotional
anxiety, she saw the hated white flag blowing down below
from the gable of the pale villa by the lake. Cheekily
jagged, the insistently tempting greeting from a corrupt
woman to the boy she wanted to ruin, it flapped up at
her. Spontaneously, as if in a threatening gesture, Beatrice
raised her hand; but then she walked quickly back into
the room, with an unconquerable urge to see her son and
talk things through with him. She put her ear to the
communicating door lest she disturb his sound sleep; and
she really felt as though she were hearing his strong and
quiet boyish breath. She now carefully opened the door,
planning to wait for Hugo to wake up and then, sitting
beside him on the divan, to ask him his secret with maternal
tenderness. But to her horror she discovered that the room
was empty. Hugo wasn't there. He had left without saying
goodbye to his mother, as once he would have done,
receiving the familiar kiss on the forehead – obviously to
avoid the question that he had seen preparing itself on
her lips for days and which she, she knew it now, would
have put to him during that quarter of an hour. So he had
come to this, driven so far from her only by his unease,
his desires. That was the result of his first handshake with
that woman, recently on the quay; of her gaze, which had
smilingly greeted him yesterday from the gallery of the

swimming pool, when his pale boy's body had emerged from the waves. Of course, he was over seventeen; and his mother had never imagined that he would save himself for someone destined for him from the beginning of eternity, who would meet him as young and pure as he was himself. She desired only this for him: that he would not waken repelled from his first intoxication, that he would not, with his fragrant youth, fall victim to the lust of a woman who owed her half-forgotten fame as an actress only to an enigmatic whorishness, and whose reputation and behaviour had not been changed by her marriage late in life.

Beatrice sat on Hugo's divan in the semi-darkness of the room, her eyes closed, her head propped in her hands, and wondered. Where could Hugo be? With the Baroness? It was unthinkable. Such things couldn't happen so quickly. But wasn't there the possibility of protecting her beloved boy against such a pitiful affair? She feared there wasn't. Because she sensed this: just as Hugo bore his father's features, his veins also ran with his blood, the dark blood of people from another, lawless world who, even as boys, glow with dark male passions, and whose eyes still flash with childhood dreams even in maturity. His father's blood alone? Was her own any more sluggish? Did she think that only because no temptation had come her way since her husband's death? And because she had never belonged to anyone else, something that she had once confessed to her husband lost some of its truth: that he alone had fulfilled her whole life because, in the depths of night when his face had darkened before her, he had always meant someone else to her, someone new – because in his arms she was the lover of King Richard and Cyrano and Hamlet and all the other roles he played: the lover of heroes and villains, the blessed and the damned, the transparent and the mysterious. Indeed, as a young girl had she not, half unconsciously, wanted the great actor as her husband because being connected to him provided her with her only chance to take the respectable course of life that seemed preordained by her conventional upbringing, and yet at the same time to lead the wild and adventurous life she longed for in her most hidden dreams? And she remembered how she had not only been able to win Ferdinand against the will of her parents, whose pious and conventional minds could never quite shake off their quiet horror of the actor even once they were married, but how she had also vanquished a much more considerable foe. When she had first met Ferdinand he had been in a well-known liaison with a rich widow past her first youth, who had done a great deal to help the young actor when he was starting out, indeed who was thought often to have paid his debts and from whom, it was said, he lacked the willpower to break away. Then Beatrice had taken the romantic decision to free this wonderful man from such unworthy bonds; and, in the kind of words that only come to one in the awareness of a moment that will never return, she had demanded that Ferdinand's ageing lover dissolve a relationship which would sooner or later have foundered on its inner untruth, perhaps too late for the well-being of the great artist and his art. She had received a mocking, wounding dismissal which she had had to bear for a long time, and it was a whole year before Ferdinand was freed once and for all; but Beatrice could never have doubted that that discussion was the original cause of his liberation, even if her husband himself had not repeatedly told the story with cheerful pride, even to people who were not involved in the slightest.

Beatrice dropped her hands from her eyes and rose from the divan, suddenly agitated. Almost twenty years lay between that bold and foolhardy step and the present; but had she become someone else in the meantime? Did she not still possess the same determination, the same courage? Could she no longer direct the fate of someone dear to her as she saw fit? Was she the woman to wait in silence until her son's young life was sullied and ruined for ever, rather than – as she had done with that other woman – confronting the Baroness, who was, after all, also a woman and who must surely, even if only in the most hidden corner of her soul, understand what it meant to be a mother? And greatly relieved by this idea she walked to the window, opened the shutters and, filled with new hope, took in the picture of the cherished landscape as if it were a message of promise. But she felt that the important thing was to turn her bold decision into action with the same confidence she had felt at the very first moment; so without further hesitation she went into her bedroom and rang for the maid, who would have to help her dress with special care today.

Once this had been taken care of to her satisfaction, she put her wide-brimmed panama hat with its narrow black band on her dark blonde, thick wavy hair, took from the vase on her bedside table the freshest of the three red roses that she had cut that morning, stuck it in her white leather belt, picked up her slender walking-stick and left the house. She felt joyful, young and certain of her case.

When she stepped outside the door the Arbesbachers were standing by the garden gate, he in his loden coat and lederhosen, about to press the bell-push, she in a dark floral calico dress which, along with her rather careworn but still rather virginal features, made her look all too matronly.

'My respects to you, *gnädige Frau*,' called the architect, raising his green hat with its chamois tuft, holding it in his hand so that his white head was uncovered for a while. 'We were just coming to get you' – and in response to her questioning look – 'have you forgotten, *gnä' Frau*? It's Thursday, cards at the bank director's house.'

'So it is,' said Beatrice, remembering.

'We've just run into your son,' the architect's wife remarked, and a tired smile crossed her faded features.

'He's off up there with two fat books,' the architect continued, pointing towards the path that led up the sunny meadow to the forest . . . 'An industrious young man.'

Beatrice smiled with an expression of disproportionate bliss. 'He graduates from school next year,' she said.

'Goodness, how lovely you're looking again today,' the architect's wife said unprompted, in a tone almost humble with admiration.

'Well, how will we feel, Beatrice,' said the architect, 'when we suddenly find ourselves with a grown-up son going to university, duelling and turning women's heads?'

'Did you duel, then?' his wife inquired.

'Well, I knocked about a bit, which comes down to much the same thing. Bloody heads one way or another!'

She walked along the path that led above the village, with the view over the lake, to the villa of Welponer the bank director.

'Yes, I'll join you,' said Beatrice, 'but I'd really like to go to the village . . . to the Post Office, there's a parcel that was sent from Vienna a week ago and still hasn't turned up. And it was sent special delivery,' she added indignantly, as though she herself believed the story she had invented on the spur of the moment, even she didn't know why.

'Your little parcel might be coming by rail,' said the architect's wife, pointing down to where the little train was just emerging, puffing and self-important, from behind the cliffs, and across the meadows to the slightly elevated station. Travellers poked their heads out of all the windows, and the architect waved his hat.

'What's up with you?' his wife said.

'We're bound to know some of them, and it's always best to be polite.'

'Goodbye, then,' said Beatrice all of a sudden. 'I'll come back up later, of course. My best wishes in the meantime.' She quickly took her leave and walked back down the path she had just climbed. She felt the architect and his wife, who had stopped where they were, watching her almost all the way to the villa that Arbesbacher had built ten years ago for his friend and hunting companion Ferdinand Heinold. Here Beatrice took the narrow track which led fairly steeply past plain country dwellings to the village, but had to wait a while before crossing the platform because the train was just leaving the station. Only now did it occur to her that she had nothing to do at the Post Office, she just wanted to speak to the Baroness, a matter that now, since she knew her boy was up in the forest with his books, no longer seemed as urgent as it had an hour before . . . She crossed the rails and found, at the station, all the confusion that follows the arrival of a train. The two coaches from the Lake Hotel and the Posthof were clattering away with their passengers; other new arrivals, followed by porters, excited and invigorated; daytrippers, carefree and good-humoured, crossed Beatrice's path. She watched with amusement as an entire family – father, mother, three children, maid and chamber-maids, with suitcases, boxes, bags, umbrellas and sticks, and a scared little Pinscher – tried to fit into a landau. From another coach a couple she had met briefly the previous year waved to her with all the boundless joy of greetings in the summer countryside. A young man wearing a light grey summer suit and carrying a very new yellow leather bag raised his straw hat to Beatrice. She didn't recognize the young man, and coolly returned his greeting.

'My respects, *gnädige Frau*,' said the stranger, sending the bag careering from one hand to the other, and rather clumsily holding out his liberated right hand to Beatrice.

'Fritz!' Beatrice cried, recognizing him.

'That's right, *gnädige Frau*, Fritzl at your service.'

'Do you know, I really didn't recognize you. You've turned into a proper dandy.'

'Oh, it's not as bad as all that,' answered Fritzl, letting the bag slip back into his other hand. 'By the way, did Hugo not get my card?'

'Your card? I don't know. But he recently told me he was expecting you.'

'Of course, people in Vienna have been talking about me coming over from Bad Ischl for a few days. But yesterday I wrote to him specially to tell him I was planning to celebrate my arrival this afternoon.'

'He'll be absolutely delighted. Where are you staying, Herr Weber?'

'No, no, *gnädige Frau*, don't call me Herr Weber.'

'So, where, Herr – Fritz?'

'I've sent my bag on to the Posthof, and as soon as I've made myself look respectable I shall take the liberty of paying a visit to Villa Beatrice.'

'Villa Beatrice? There isn't such a thing for miles around.'

'So what is it called if someone with such a lovely name lives in it?'

'It isn't called anything. I can't bear such things. It's No. 7 Eichwiesenweg; you see, the one over there with the little green balcony.'

Fritz Weber looked reverently in the direction suggested. 'It must have a lovely view. But I shan't dawdle any longer. I hope I'll find Hugo at home in an hour's time?'

'I think so. At the moment he's up in the forest studying.'

'Studying? We'll have to wean him off that pretty quickly.'

'Oh, will you now!'

'I want to go hiking with him. Did you know, *gnädige Frau*, that I was on the Dachstein recently?'

'Sadly no, Herr Weber, there was no mention of it in the local newspaper.'

'I beg you, *gnädige Frau*, not Herr Weber.'

'I think we'll have to stick to it, since I have the honour of being neither your aunt nor your governess . . .'

'It would be delightful to have such an aunt.'

'So, he's gallant as well – my goodness!' She laughed out loud: suddenly before her, in place of the elegant young gentleman, was the boy she had known since he was twelve, and his little blond moustache looked as though it were stuck on.

'Goodbye, then, Fritzl,' she said, and reached out her hand in farewell. 'This evening at dinner you'll tell us more about your outing to the Dachstein, won't you?'

Fritz bowed rather stiffly, then kissed Beatrice's hand, which she allowed him to do, submitting to the swift passing of the years; finally he disappeared with a heightened confidence expressed in his posture and his gait. And that, thought Beatrice, is a friend of my Hugo. Of course, he's a little older than my son, by one and a half or two years at least. And he was in a higher class at school. Beatrice remembered that he had once had to repeat a year. But she was pleased that he was here and planned to go on hikes with Hugo. But if only she could send the two boys off on outings lasting a week or a fortnight! Ten hours' hard march, with the mountain wind blowing around their brows, in the evening collapsing exhausted on the straw and setting off hiking again with the morning sun – how lovely, how healthy that would be! She felt a certain desire to go with them. But that was out of the question. The boys wouldn't want an aunt or a governess tagging along. She sighed quietly and ran her hand over her forehead.

She continued walking on the country road along the lakeside. The little steamer had just left the landing stage, and was floating, white and pretty, diagonally across the water to the Lea, as it was known, with the few quiet houses hidden beneath chestnut trees and fruit trees, where the natural world was already getting ready for the evening. On the diving board in the swimming pool a figure in a white dressing-gown was bobbing up and down. There were still a few people swimming in the lake. They're better off than I am, thought Beatrice, and looked enviously at the water, from which a cooling, peaceful breeze wafted up to her. But she quickly brushed aside the temptation and, independent and determined, continued on her way until she found herself almost accidentally in front of the villa where Baroness Fortunata was staying that summer. From the veranda that ran along the front of the house, over the medium-sized front garden, bright with blossoming hollyhocks and stocks, pale clothes shimmered. Without a sideways glance Beatrice continued walking along the white fence. To her shame she felt her heart beating more loudly. The sound of two women's voices reached her ear; Beatrice quickened her step, and suddenly she was past the house. She decided, for the time being, to go up into the village, to the grocer's where she often needed to get something, and as she certainly did today, when they had a guest for dinner. A few minutes later she was standing in Anton Meissenbichler's shop, buying cold meat, fruit and cheese, and giving little Loisl a tip and the task of bringing the package straight up to Eichwiesenweg. But what now? she asked herself, when she was standing outside in the church square, opposite the open cemetery gate, watching the gilded crosses shimmering red in the evening sun. Should she simply abandon her plan because her heart had been beating faster than usual? She would never have forgiven herself such weakness. And fate, she felt, would surely have punished her. So there was nothing for it but to go back – and to see the Baroness without further delay.

A few minutes later Beatrice was down at the shore. Now past the Lake Hotel, on whose capacious raised terrace summer guests were sitting over coffee and ice-cream, then past the two new massive modern villas that she couldn't stand; and two seconds later her eyes met those of the Baroness, who was lying under a huge white-and-red-spotted parasol on a wicker lounger on the veranda. Leaning against the wall was a second lady with an ivory-yellowish face, like a statue, in a flowing white tunic. Fortunata had just been talking animatedly, yet now she suddenly fell silent and her features stiffened; but they immediately relaxed again, her whole face became a smile, a greeting, her expression a real glow of warmth and welcome. You fraud! thought Beatrice, somewhat indignant at her own phrase, and felt forearmed. And Fortunata's voice rang in her ear with excessive cheerfulness: 'Good-day, Frau Heinold.'

'Good-day,' Beatrice replied, her voice barely raised, as if she didn't much care whether her greeting was heard on the veranda or not; and made as if to go on walking.

But Fortunata called across to her: 'I expect you're planning a sun and dust bath today, Frau Heinold.' Beatrice was in no doubt: Fortunata had only said that in order to start a conversation with her. For the acquaintance between the two women was so superficial that the jocular tone did not even seem especially appropriate. Many years before, at a theatre festival, Beatrice had met Fortunata Schön, a colleague of Ferdinand Heinold, and in the ease of the evening's merriment the couple had dined and drunk champagne at the same table as Fortunata and her then lover. Later they had met fleetingly in the theatre and on the street, but they had never had real conversations of more than a few moments. Eight years previously, after her marriage to the Baron, Fortunata had left the stage and vanished completely from Beatrice's sight, until she had spotted her again by chance a few weeks previously at the swimming pool. From that meeting onwards she had exchanged only a few words with her, since this could hardly be avoided, in the street, in the forest, at the pool. But today it suited Beatrice that the Baroness herself seemed inclined to begin a conversation, so she replied, as naturally as possible: 'Sunbathing? The sun has gone – and by the lake in the evening it isn't as sultry as it is up in the forest.'

Fortunata had risen to her feet; with her slender but very shapely little figure, she leaned against the balustrade and replied rather hastily that she, for her part, preferred walks in the forest – she particularly found the one to the hermitage really quite captivating. What a stupid word, thought Beatrice, and politely asked why the Baroness, if that was her preference, had not moved into one of the villas at the forest's edge. The Baroness explained that she, or rather her husband, had rented this villa down here in response to an advertisement; and in any case she was content in every respect. 'But won't you come, *gnädige Frau*,' she hurriedly added, 'and take tea with my friend and me?' And without waiting for an answer she walked towards Beatrice, stretched out a slender, white, somewhat unsteady hand and guided her with exaggerated friendliness on to the veranda, where the other lady was still leaning motionlessly against the wall in her flowing white muslin tunic, with a kind of grim seriousness that struck Beatrice as half weird and half ludicrous. Fortunata introduced her: 'Fräulein Wilhelmine Fallehn – Frau Beatrice Heinold. You must be familiar with the name, my dear Willy.'

'I had no end of admiration for your husband,' Fräulein Fallehn said coolly, in a dark voice.

Fortunata showed Beatrice to an upholstered wicker chair and apologized for immediately lying down again just as comfortably as before. Never, in fact, had she felt so tired, utterly drained, as she did here, particularly during the afternoon. It might be due to the fact that she couldn't resist the temptation of bathing twice every day, each time staying in the water for a full hour. But only if you knew as many kinds of water as she did, inland lakes and rivers and seas, only then did you discover that each kind of water has, to an extent, its own character. She went on talking in this manner, elegant and overly refined as it seemed to Beatrice; and from time to time, as though exhausted, she ran one hand over her reddish dyed hair. Her long white housecoat, trimmed with pillow lace, hung to the floor on both sides of the low lounger. Around her bare neck she wore a modest string of small pearls. Her pale, slender face was heavily powdered; only the tip of her nose had a reddish shimmer, and her distinctly made-up lips were dark red. Beatrice couldn't help calling to mind a picture from an illustrated newspaper showing a Pierrot dangling from a lamp-post, an impression reinforced for her by the fact that Fortunata tended to keep her eyes half closed when she spoke.

Tea and cakes were brought, the conversation got under way, and Wilhelmine Fallehn, who, more informal than before, was leaning against the balustrade with her cup in her hand, joined in; their talk took them from summer to winter, they spoke of the city, the state of the theatre, the insignificant successors of Ferdinand Heinold and the terribly premature death of the unforgotten actor. In an even tone Wilhelmine expressed her astonishment that a woman could possibly survive the loss of such a man, whereupon the Baroness, aware of Beatrice's unease, simply observed: 'You should know, Willy, that Frau Heinold has a son.'

At that moment Beatrice looked with uncontrolled hostility into her eyes, which returned her gaze like a mocking water-sprite; yes, it almost seemed to Beatrice as if Fortunata exuded a damp scent of reeds and water-lilies. At the same time she noticed that Fortunata's feet were bare in their sandals, and that she was naked beneath her white linen dress. But meanwhile the Baroness went on talking quite naturally, in a suave and cultured manner; she claimed that life was stronger than death, and that life must consequently be right in the end; but Beatrice felt that she was being addressed by a creature whose beloved had never died, indeed by a person who had never really loved anyone, man or woman.

Wilhelmine Fallehn suddenly put down her cup. 'I've got to finish packing,' she explained, briefly said her goodbyes and disappeared through the drawing-room overlooking the garden.

'My friend is leaving for Vienna today,' said Fortunata. 'She's engaged – so to speak.'

'Ah,' said Beatrice politely.

'What do you think she is?' asked Fortunata with half-closed eyes.

'I should imagine she's an artist?'

Fortunata shook her head. 'She was with the theatre for a while, though. She's the daughter of a high-ranking officer. Or rather, his orphan. Her father put a bullet in his head out of shame at her change of career. Ten years ago. She's twenty-seven now. She'll go far. Will you have another cup of tea?'

'No, thank you, Baroness.' She took a deep breath. Her moment had come. All at once her features tensed so resolutely that Fortunata involuntarily sat half upright. And Beatrice decisively began, 'I didn't walk past your house by chance. I have something to discuss with you, Baroness.'

'Oh,' said Fortunata, and a slight blush appeared beneath her powdered Pierrot face. She leaned one arm on the support of her lounger and intertwined her restless fingers.

'Let me be brief,' Beatrice began.

'Exactly as you wish. As brief or as long as you want, my dear Frau Heinold.'

Beatrice was irritated by this somewhat condescending form of address and replied rather sharply, 'Briefly and simply, Baroness, I don't want my son to become your lover.'

She was completely calm; in fact she had felt exactly as she had nineteen years before, when she had demanded her future husband from an ageing widow.

The Baroness returned Beatrice's cool gaze just as calmly. 'So,' she said, half to herself, 'you don't want that? – What a shame. However, to tell the truth it's never even occurred to me.'

'So it will be all the easier for you,' Beatrice answered a little hoarsely, 'to grant my wish.'

'Yes, if it was up to me alone –'

'Baroness, it is entirely up to you. You know that very well. My son is still practically a child.'

A painful tension appeared around Fortunata's made-up lips. 'What a dangerous woman I must be,' she began thoughtfully. 'Shall I tell you why my friend is leaving? She was really to have spent the whole summer with me – and her fiancé was to visit her here. And just think, she suddenly got frightened, frightened of me. Then again, perhaps she's right. That's just the way I am. I'm really not responsible for myself.'

Beatrice sat there stiffly. Such candour, almost shamelessness, was not what she had expected. And she answered acidly, 'Well, Baroness, if that's your way of thinking, you wouldn't have too many qualms if my son were to –' She stopped.

Fortunata cast a childlike gaze at Beatrice: 'What you are doing here, Frau Heinold,' she said in what sounded like a new tone of voice, 'is actually quite touching. But clever, goodness me, clever it isn't. Incidentally, I may repeat that I haven't even remotely thought about . . . Really, Frau Heinold, I think women like you have the wrong idea about women – of my kind. You see, two years ago, for example, I spent three whole months in a Dutch fishing village – utterly alone. And I don't think I've ever been so happy in my whole life. And equally it could have happened that this summer too – oh, I still wouldn't like to rule it out. I've never made resolutions, never in my life. Even my marriage, I assure you, was pure chance.' And she looked up as though an idea had suddenly occurred to her. 'Oh, are you afraid of the Baron? Are you worried that your – your dear son might attract some kind of unpleasantness from that quarter – as far as that's concerned . . .' And she closed her eyes with a smile.

Beatrice shook her head. 'I haven't really thought of dangers from that quarter.'

'Well, you might just bear it in mind. Husbands can be unpredictable. But you see, Frau Heinold' – and she opened her eyes again – 'if that consideration really did have nothing to do with it, then I find the whole thing even more incomprehensible – quite seriously. For example if I had a son the age of your Hugo –'

'You know his name?' Beatrice asked severely.

Fortunata smiled. 'You told me his name yourself. Just recently, on the jetty.'

'Quite right. Forgive me, Baroness.'

'As, dear Frau Heinold, I was about to say: if *I* had a son and he fell in love, for example, with a woman like you, I don't know – I don't think I can imagine a better début for a young person.'

Beatrice moved her chair as though to rise to her feet.

'Here we are women together,' Fortunata said soothingly.

'You have no son, Baroness . . . and then –' She stopped.

'I see, you think that would make something of a difference. Perhaps it would. But that difference would only make the matter – for my son – all the more disturbing. Because you, Frau Heinold, would probably take such an issue seriously. On the other hand, as for me – me! Yes, really, the more I think about it, Frau Heinold, it would have been cleverer of you to come to me with the opposite request. If you had' – and she smiled with half-closed eyes – 'had, so to speak, entrusted your son to me.'

'Baroness!' Beatrice was stunned. She could have screamed.

Fortunata leaned back, crossed her arms beneath her head and completely closed her eyes. 'Such things do happen.' And she began to tell a story. 'Some years ago – unfortunately a good many years ago now, somewhere in the provinces, there was a fellow actress who was then about the same age as I am now. She played heroic and sentimental roles. One day she had a visit from Countess . . . well, the name is irrelevant . . . Well, her son, the young Count, had fallen in love with a middle-class girl of good but rather poor family. Civil servants or something. And the young Count had his heart set on marrying the girl. He wasn't yet twenty. And his mother the Countess – do you know what the clever lady did? One fine day she appears at my colleague's home and talks to her . . . and asks her . . . Well – to cut a long story short she arranges for her son to forget the middle-class girl in my colleague's arms and –'

'I should prefer you to refrain from telling me such anecdotes, Baroness.'

'It isn't an anecdote. It's a true story and a very moral one to boot. A misalliance was prevented, an unhappy marriage, perhaps even a suicide or a double suicide.'

'Perhaps,' said Beatrice. 'But none of that has anything to do with the matter at hand. I'm not like that countess. And as far as I'm concerned the thought is simply unbearable . . . unbearable . . .'

Fortunata smiled and remained silent for a while, as if she wanted to force the sentence to its conclusion. Then she said, 'Your son is sixteen . . . or seventeen?'

'Seventeen,' replied Beatrice, immediately annoyed with herself for supplying the information so obediently.

Fortunata lowered her eyes and seemed to abandon herself to some kind of vision. And she said as if from a dream, 'You'll have to get used to the idea. If it isn't me, it'll be someone else. – And who can promise you' – a green glow came from her suddenly opened eyes – 'that it will be someone better?'

'Please, Baroness,' Beatrice replied with hard-won superiority, 'let me worry about that.'

Fortunata sighed quietly. She suddenly seemed tired and said, 'Fine, what more is there to say? I should like to oblige you. So, your dear son has nothing to fear from me – or, as one might also see it, to hope from me . . . If you are not' – and now her eyes grew large, grey and clear – 'on completely the wrong track, Frau Heinold. Because for myself, to be quite honest, you see, I hadn't been previously aware that Hugo' – she let the name slowly fade on her tongue – 'was particularly impressed by me.' And she looked Beatrice innocently in the face. Beatrice, who had turned dark red, held her lips pressed silently together. 'So, what am I to do? I could write to my husband and tell him that the air here doesn't agree with me. What do you think, Frau Heinold?'

Beatrice shrugged her shoulders. 'If you really want, I mean, if you wished to be so kind as . . . not to concern yourself with my son . . . it won't be so hard, Baroness, your word would be enough for me.'

'My word? Do you not consider, Frau Heinold, that in such matters words and solemn promises, oh, even from women unlike my own kind, have very little meaning?'

'You don't love him,' Beatrice suddenly exclaimed, entirely without restraint. 'It would be a whim and nothing more. And I'm his mother, Baroness. You'll not have allowed me to take such a step in vain.'

Fortunata rose to her feet, took a long look at Beatrice, and then reached out her hand. She seemed suddenly to have put all her reservations behind her. 'From this moment onwards your dear son has ceased to exist,' she said gravely. 'Forgive me for making you wait so long for this – obvious answer.'

Beatrice took her hand and in that moment she felt sympathy, even a kind of pity, for the Baroness. She almost felt tempted to take her leave with a word of apology. But she suppressed that impulse, even avoided expressing anything that might have sounded like gratitude, and only said, somewhat helplessly, 'Well, then, everything is fine, Baroness.' And rose to her feet.

'You're going so soon?' asked Fortunata courteously.

'I have detained you long enough,' Beatrice replied similarly.

Fortunata smiled, and Beatrice felt rather stupid. She allowed the Baroness to accompany her to the garden gate, and reached out her hand to her once more. 'Thank

you for your visit,' Fortunata said very charmingly, add-
ing, 'If I don't find myself returning it in the immediate
future, I hope you won't think it ill of me.'

'Oh,' said Beatrice, and from the street she returned
the friendly nod of the Baroness, who had stopped at the
garden gate. Beatrice involuntarily walked more quickly
than usual, and kept to the level country road; later she
would be able to turn off into the narrow forest path that
led steep and straight to the bank director's villa. What
is the state of things now? she wondered agitatedly. Did
I emerge the victor? She gave me her word, after all. But
didn't she herself say that women's promises don't mean
much? No, she won't dare. She's seen now what I'm
capable of. Fortunata's words went on echoing within
her. How strangely she had spoken of that summer in
Holland! As if of relaxing, heaving a sigh of relief after a
wild and sweet but difficult time. And she suddenly imagined Fortunata, the white linen dress over her naked body,
running along a beach as if hounded by evil spirits. Perhaps
it wasn't always pleasant to be a creature of the kind that
Fortunata certainly was. In a sense she was probably, like
many women of her sort, inwardly destroyed, insane and
barely responsible for the harm she did. No, she could do
what she liked as long as she left Hugo in peace. Did he
have to be the one? And Beatrice smiled when it occurred
to her that one might have offered the Baroness, as a kind
of substitute, a new arrival, a handsome young gentleman
called Fritz Weber, with whom she would have been perfectly happy. Yes, she should have suggested that. Really,
that would have given a little spice to that delightful conversation. What kinds of women there were! What kinds of
lives they led! The kind of lives from which they had to
recover from time to time in Dutch fishing villages. For still

others, their whole lives *were* such a Dutch fishing village. And Beatrice smiled, without feeling especially cheerful.

She arrived at the park gate of the Welponers' villa and walked in. From the tennis court quite near the entrance, through the thin shrubs, Beatrice saw the glimmer of white costumes, heard the familiar cries and walked closer. Two pairs of brothers and sisters stood facing one another: the son and daughter of the house, nineteen and eighteen years old, both like their father, their features and gestures betraying their Italian–Jewish origins; on the other side Dr Bertram and his excessively slim sister Leonie, the children of a famous doctor who had a villa here in the village. At first Beatrice stood some distance away, delighting in the powerfully free movement of the young forms, the keen flight of the balls, and felt agreeably fanned by the fresh gust of a sweet and pointless competition. The set ended after a few minutes. The two couples, rackets in their hands, met at the net and stayed there, chatting; their faces, previously tense with the excitement of the game, blurred in a kind of empty smile, their glances, which had just been fixed on the balls' trajectories, dipped softly into one another; strangely, almost painfully, Beatrice felt the atmosphere, so pure before, growing steamy and forming storm clouds, and it made her think: how would this evening end if all of a sudden, through some miracle, all the rules of morality were abolished from the world, and these young people were able to follow unhindered their secret urges, of which perhaps even they were unaware? And suddenly it occurred to her that such lawless worlds did exist; that she herself had risen from just such a world, and still bore its scent in her hair. Only for that reason did she now see what had otherwise always escaped her innocent eyes. Only for that reason? Had she not once been mysteriously familiar with those worlds? Had she not herself been the lover of the blessed and the damned . . . the transparent and the mysterious . . . of criminals and heroes . . . ?

She had been noticed. She was greeted with a wave of the hand; she walked closer to the wire fence, the others walked to her, and a casual conversation went back and forth. But she felt as if the two young men were looking at her as they had never looked at her before. Young Dr Bertram in particular had a kind of supercilious mockery playing around his lips, and let his eyes slide up and down her as he had never done, or as she had never noticed. And when she said goodbye, finally to go up to the villa, he jokingly took one of her fingers through the wire fence and pressed upon it a kiss that seemed as though it would never end. And he laughed cheekily when dark wrinkles of displeasure appeared on her brow.

Up on the covered, rather over-grand terrace, Beatrice found the two couples, the Welponers and the Arbesbachers, at their card-game. She refused to disturb them, and, when she saw that the bank director was about to put his cards down, she pushed him back into this chair and then took a seat between him and his wife. She wanted to watch the game, she said, but she barely did so and was soon gazing across the stone balustrade to the edges of the mountains on which the sun's last gleams were fading. Here a feeling of security and belonging came over her, which she hadn't felt with the young people outside – which calmed her and at the same time made her feel sad. The bank director's wife offered her tea in that rather condescending way that one had to get used to every time. Beatrice remembered she'd just had tea a moment before. Just a moment before? How many miles away was the house with the cheekily jagged flag! How many hours or days had it taken her to get from there to here! Shadows were falling over the park, the sun vanished suddenly from the mountains, vague sounds rose from the road below, which couldn't be seen from here. All of a sudden Beatrice felt as lonely as she had felt at dusk in the country very shortly after Ferdinand's death, and afterwards never again. Hugo too had suddenly vanished into unreality, where he was unreachably remote. She was seized by a truly painful longing for him, and she hastily took leave of the party. The bank director would not be deterred from accompanying her. He walked down the broad steps with her, then back along the pond at whose centre the fountain slept, then past the tennis court where the brothers and sisters went on playing so eagerly, despite the darkening evening, that they didn't notice the woman walking past. The bank director cast a gloomy glance in that direction, and it was not the first time that Beatrice had noticed him doing so. But she felt as if she were understanding that too for the first time. She knew that the bank director, in the midst of his strenuous and successful activity as a bold man of finance, was touched by the melancholy of ageing. And while he walked by her side, his tall figure a little bowed only as if out of affectation, and carrying on a light conversation with her, about the wonderful summer weather and all kinds of outings that they should really take and which one never got round to taking, Beatrice repeatedly felt that something was weaving back and forth between the two of them, like invisible autumnal threads; and when he kissed her hand as she left him at the park gate, he brought to it a chivalrous melancholy whose echoes accompanied her all the way home.

At the door the serving-girl told her that Hugo and another young gentleman were in the garden, and also that the postman had brought a parcel. Beatrice found it lying in her room and smiled with satisfaction. Did fate not mean her well, in turning her trivial little lie into a truth? Or was it more of a warning: you're getting away with it this time? The parcel came from Dr Teichmann. It contained books he had promised to send her: memoirs and letters from great statesmen and generals, characters for whom the little lawyer, as Beatrice knew, had the highest admiration. Beatrice momentarily immersed herself in the study of the title pages, took her hat off in her bedroom, put a shawl around her shoulders and went into the garden. Down by the fence she saw the boys, who, without noticing her, kept jumping repeatedly into the air as though they had gone mad. As Beatrice approached she saw that they had both removed their jackets. Now Hugo ran up to her and kissed her, for the first time in weeks, childishly and impetuously on both cheeks. Fritz hurried to slip into his jacket, bowed and kissed Beatrice's hand. She smiled. She felt as though he wanted to blow away that other melancholy kiss with the touch of his young lips.

'So, what are you up to?' asked Beatrice.

'Seeing who can win the world high-jump championship,' explained Fritz.

The tall heads of corn beyond the fence swayed in the evening wind. Down below, the lake lay dull grey and lifeless. 'You could put your jacket on too, Hugo,' said Beatrice, tenderly brushing his damp blond hair from his forehead. Hugo obeyed. Beatrice was struck that her boy looked rather inelegant and boyish compared with his friend, but at the same time she was agreeably touched by the fact. 'Just think, Mother,' said Hugo, 'Fritz wants to get the eight thirty train back to Ischl.'

'Why is that?'

'No room to be had, *gnädige Frau*. Perhaps one will come free in two or three days.'

'You're not going back just because of that, Herr Fritz? We have room for you.'

'I told him, Mother, that you would have no objections.'

'What objections could I have? Of course you can stay upstairs in the guest-room. What else is it for?'

'*Gnädige Frau*, I have no desire to put anyone out. I know how furious my own mama gets when we have people to stay in Ischl.'

'It's different with us, Herr Fritz.'

And they agreed that young Herr Weber's luggage would be fetched up from the Posthof, where it was in temporary storage, and that for the time being he would stay in the attic, in return for which Beatrice solemnly pledged to call him simply 'Fritz', without the 'Herr'.

Beatrice gave the staff the necessary instructions and thought it appropriate to leave the young people to themselves for a time, only reappearing at dinner in the conservatory. For the first time in many days Hugo was naturally jolly; and Fritz too had stopped playing the adult young gentleman. Two schoolboys sat at the table, as usual beginning by gossiping about their professors, then talking matter-of-factly about the prospects for the next, final school year, and finally about more distant plans for the future. Fritz Weber, who wanted to become a doctor, had, he said, visited the dissecting room once during the previous winter, and hinted that other secondary school-boys would hardly be a match for such powerful impressions. Hugo, for his part, had decided long ago to devote himself to archaeology. He was the owner of a small collection of antiques: a Pompeiian lamp, a little piece of mosaic from the baths of Caracalla, a pistol lock from the time of the French occupation and other things of that sort. He also planned to begin excavations here by the lake, at the Lea, where remnants of pile dwellings were thought to have been found. Fritz made no secret of his doubts as to the authenticity of Hugo's museum pieces. That pistol lock in particular, which Hugo had personally found on the Turkish entrenchments around Vienna, had always struck him as suspicious. Beatrice thought Fritz was still too young for such scepticism, to which he replied that it had nothing to do with age, it was a matter of temperament. I prefer my Hugo, Beatrice thought, to this precocious rascal. Certainly, it will be harder for him. She looked at him. His eyes gazed into some distant place where Fritz certainly couldn't follow him. Beatrice went on thinking: of course he has no idea what kind of person that Fortunata is. Who knows what he's imagining. As far as he's concerned she may be a kind of fairy-tale princess being held prisoner by a wicked magician. How he sits there now with his tousled blond hair and his disorderly tie. And it's still the mouth he had as a child, that full, red, sweet child's mouth! Certainly, his father had it too. He'd always had that child's mouth and those child's eyes. And she looked out into the darkness that lay over the meadow, as heavy and black as though the forest itself had moved just outside the window.

'Is smoking permitted?' Fritz asked. Beatrice nodded, whereupon Fritz brought out a silver cigarette case with a golden monogram and charmingly offered it to the lady of the house. Beatrice took a cigarette and a light and learned that Fritz got his tobacco directly from Alexandria.

Hugo was smoking today as well. It was, he admitted, precisely the seventh cigarette of his life. Fritz had long since stopped being able to count his. Incidentally, the case had been a present from his father, who fortunately had progressive opinions, and he reported the latest: his sister was going to graduate from secondary school in three years and probably study medicine, just like himself. Beatrice cast a swift glance at Hugo, who was blushing slightly. Was it, in the end, still the love of little Elise that he bore in his heart – and which was responsible for the painful tension around his lips? 'Couldn't we go for another row?' Fritz asked. 'It's such a lovely night, and so warm.'

'Better to wait for moonlight,' said Beatrice. 'It's too frightening to go out on the water when the nights are so dark.'

'That's what I think as well,' said Hugo. Fritz twitched his nostrils contemptuously. But then the boys agreed that they wanted to eat ice-cream at the day's end on the terrace of the Lake Hotel.

'Rogues,' Beatrice joked as they left.

Then she checked that everything was in order in the attic, and, as she always did, tidied up in the house a little. Finally she went to her bedroom, undressed and lay down in bed. Soon she heard a clatter and a man's voice outside; clearly the porter had brought Fritz's luggage, which was now being carried up the wooden steps. Then there was whispering between the porter and the chambermaid, which lasted longer than was strictly necessary; finally it was quiet. Beatrice took one of the heroic books that Teichmann had sent and began to read the memoirs of a French cavalry general. But her mind wasn't on it, she was uneasy and tired at the same time. She felt as though it was the deep silence around her that wasn't letting her sleep. After some time she heard the front door opening, shortly afterwards quiet steps, whispering, laughter. It was the boys! They were trying to get up the stairs as silently as possible. Then, from above, came a shuffle, a creak, a whisper; then, again, muted steps down the stairs. That was Hugo, going to his room to sleep. And now everything in the house was still. Beatrice put her book aside, turned off the light and went to sleep reassured, almost happy.

Chapter Two

Now they had finally reached their destination. It had, it was generally established, taken longer than the architect had calculated. He disagreed. 'What'd I say? Three hours from Eichwiesenweg. It's hardly my fault we set off at nine rather than eight.' 'But it's half past one,' remarked Fritz. 'Yes, when it comes to calculating time,' the architect's wife said sadly, 'he's quite unique.' 'When ladies are involved,' her husband explained, 'you always have to add on fifty per cent. Even when you go shopping with them, everyone knows that.' And he gave a booming laugh.

Young Dr Bertram, who had stayed near Beatrice since the beginning of the excursion, spread out his green coat on the meadow. 'Please, *gnädige Frau*,' he said, gesturing down to it with an elegant smile. His words and looks had been highly suggestive since he had kissed Beatrice's finger through the tennis court fence. 'No, thank you,' Beatrice replied, 'I'm well provided for.' And, at a glance from her, with a bold flourish Fritz rolled out the tartan plaid that he was carrying on his arm. But the wind swept so strongly over the alpine pasture that the plaid flapped like a massive veil; until Beatrice caught it by its other end and spread it out with Fritz's help.

'It's always so windy up here,' said the architect. 'But

it's nice, isn't it?' And he gestured around him with a broad wave of his hand.

They were on a great expanse of mown meadow which, falling away evenly, provided a view in every direction. They looked all around and fell silent for a while in appreciative contemplation. The gentlemen had taken off their loden hats: Hugo's hair was even more unruly than usual, the tips of the architect's white hair, sticking straight up, moved in the wind, and even Fritz's well-groomed hairstyle suffered somewhat, with only Bertram's combed-down, light blond head immune to the wind that blew tirelessly over the hill. Arbesbacher named the individual peaks, gave their various altitudes and identified a rock beyond the lake that had never been climbed from the north. Bertram remarked that this was an error; he himself had climbed the north face the previous year.

'Then you must have been the first,' said the architect.

'That's possible,' replied Bertram casually, immediately calling attention to another peak which looked much less threatening, and which he had not yet dared to attempt. He knew precisely, he said, how far he could go; he wasn't at all foolhardy, and had considerable objections where death was concerned. He uttered the word 'death' quite lightly, like an expert who scorns the idea of boasting in front of a group of laymen.

Beatrice had stretched herself out on the tartan plaid and looked up at the dull blue sky, where thin white summer clouds drifted gently. She knew that Bertram was speaking for her benefit, and that he was spreading out all his interesting qualities, pride and modesty, contempt for death and instinct for life, to some extent for her to choose. But it had not the slightest effect on her.

The youngest members of the outing, Fritz and Hugo,

had brought the supplies in their rucksacks. Leonie had helped them pack, and also spread butter on the sandwiches, ladylike and maternal, although only after she had taken off her yellow gloves and stuck them in her brown leather belt. The architect uncorked the bottles. Bertram poured the wine, handed the ladies the filled glasses and looked past Beatrice, with wilful absent-mindedness, to the unconquerable peak beyond the lake. And they all thought it wonderful that, up there, with the mountain wind blowing around them, they could indulge in sandwiches and sharp Terlaner wine. The meal concluded with a tart that Frau Welponer, the bank director's wife, had sent Beatrice that morning, apologizing that she and her family could sadly not come on the outing to which she had been so looking forward. Her negative reply was not unexpected. Enticing the Welponer family from their park was gradually becoming a problem, as Leonie claimed. The architect reminded them that the esteemed guests who were present should not overestimate their own enterprising natures. How, after all, did people spend the lovely summertime? They dawdled around, as he put it, on the forest paths, they swam in the lake, played tennis and cards; but how many preliminary discussions and preparations had it taken before they finally decided, after such a long time, to climb up to the alpine pasture, a feat that could only really be described as a walk!

Beatrice thought to herself that she had only ever been up here once before – with Ferdinand, ten years ago, in the same summer that they had moved into the newly built villa. But she couldn't grasp that this was the same meadow where she was lying now: she had stored it in her memory as completely different, more expansive and brighter. A gentle sadness crept into her heart. How alone she was among all these people. What could all this surrounding merriment and chat mean to her? They were all lying on the meadow, clinking glasses. Fritz touched his glass against Beatrice's; but then, when she had long since drained her own, he kept his motionlessly in his hand and stared at her. What an expression! thought Beatrice. Even more enraptured and hungry than the looks he has been sending me at home over the past few days. Or does it seem that way to me because I've just drunk three glasses of wine one after another? She stretched out once again on her plaid, beside the architect's wife, now almost asleep, squinted into the air and saw a narrow little cloud of smoke rising elegantly upwards – from Bertram's cigarette, which she couldn't see. But she sensed his gaze creeping along her to the nape of her neck, where she thought she could physically feel it for a moment, until she finally realized that she was being tickled by a blade of grass. As if from a long way off she heard the voice of the architect, telling the boys about the time before the little railway had been built; and, although less than fifteen years had passed since then, he was able to envelop that period in an atmosphere of hoary old age. Among other things he talked of a drunken coachman who had driven him into the lake in those days, and whom he had almost beaten to death. Then Fritz related a heroic deed: in the Vienna Woods he had recently sent an extremely dubious young man packing by reaching into his pocket as though he kept his revolver there. Because what counted was presence of mind, he said by way of explanation, not the revolver. 'It's just a shame,' said the architect, 'that you haven't always got a chamberful of presence of mind about your person.' The boys laughed. How well Beatrice knew that warm, double-voiced laugh that had delighted her so often at home: and how pleased she was that the boys were so very well behaved. Recently they had even been away for two days, well equipped, on a trip to the Gosau lakes, in preparation for the September hike they had planned. Admittedly, they had been closer friends in Vienna than Beatrice had been aware. So it had been news to her, which Hugo had foolishly kept silent, to discover that among other things the two of them sometimes went to play billiards in a suburban coffee-house after gym practice. But in any case she was profoundly grateful to Fritz for coming here. Hugo was once again as fresh and natural as ever, the painful tension had vanished from his face, and he must certainly have stopped thinking of the dangerous lady with the Pierrot face and the red-dyed hair. And Beatrice could certainly not deny that the lady was behaving blamelessly. Only a few days before, by chance, she had been standing beside Beatrice in the gallery of the swimming pool just as Hugo and Fritz, for a bet as usual, were swimming over from the lake; they reached the slippery jetty at the same time, each holding on with one arm, each spraying water in the other's face, laughed, plunged beneath the surface and emerged again quite a way out. Fortunata, wrapped in her white dressing-gown, had watched briefly, with an absent-minded smile, as if observing children at play, and then looked out again over the lake, with lost, sad eyes, making Beatrice remember, with quiet unease, almost guiltily, that curious and still somewhat wounding conversation in the white-flagged villa, which the Baroness herself had clearly already forgotten and forgiven. Once in the evening, on a bench by the forest's edge, Beatrice had also seen the Baron, who had probably come visiting for only a few days. He had light blond hair, his face beardless and furrowed but still young, steely-grey eyes; he wore a light blue flannel suit and smoked a short pipe, and next to him on the bench was his sailor's cap. To Beatrice he looked like a captain who had come from far-off lands and would soon have to go back to sea. Fortunata sat beside him, small, well mannered, her reddish nose pointing forwards, her arms tired: like a puppet that the captain from over the sea could fetch from the cupboard at will and then hang up again.

All of this passed through Beatrice's head as she lay on the meadow of the alpine pasture, the wind blowing through her hair and blades of grass tickling the nape of her neck. All around it was quite silent now, everyone seemed to have fallen asleep; only some distance away someone was whistling very quietly. Spontaneously, her eyes squinting, Beatrice looked again for the elegant little cloud of smoke and soon discovered it, rising upwards, thin and silver-grey. Beatrice raised her head very slightly, and saw Bertram, his head resting on both arms and his gaze fixed eagerly on Beatrice's *décolletage*. He was also talking, and it was not impossible that he had been talking for some time, perhaps even that his speech had woken Beatrice from her half-sleep. He was asking her whether she felt like taking part on a real mountain hike, proper rock-climbing, or whether she was afraid of heights; it didn't have to be a rock, by the way, he'd be happy with some plateau or other; it just had to be higher than this, much higher, so that the others couldn't come with them. Alone with her, looking down from a peak into the valley – he imagined that would be magnificent. As he received no answer, he asked, 'Well, Frau Beatrice?' 'I'm asleep,' answered Beatrice. 'Then let me be your dream, *gnädige Frau*', he began and went on talking quietly: that there was no finer death than through falling into the abyss; your whole life passed before you in terrible clarity, and of course that would be more delightful the more beautiful things one had experienced in the past; and one didn't feel the slightest fear, just an unimaginable tension, a kind of . . . yes, a kind of metaphysical curiosity. And with rapid fingers he buried his extinguished cigarette butt in the soil. And anyway, he continued, he wasn't keen on falling, quite the contrary. Because he, who had had to witness so many dark and terrible things in the course of his profession, valued everything that was light and lovely in life all the more. And would Beatrice perhaps like to take a look at the hospital garden? A very strange atmosphere hung around it, especially on autumn evenings. He himself now lived in the hospital. And if Beatrice would like to take the opportunity to have tea with him –

'You've gone mad,' said Beatrice, sat up and looked around with clear eyes into the blue-gold brightness that seemed to swallow the dull lines of the mountains. Sun-drenched, very wide awake, she rose to her feet, shook her dress and realized as she did so that she was, quite against her will, looking down encouragingly at Bertram. She rapidly looked away, to Leonie, who was standing alone some way off, picturesque, a floating veil wrapped around her head. The architect and the boys, sitting legs crossed on the meadow, were playing cards. 'Soon you won't have to give Hugo pocket money, *gnä' Frau*,' called the architect, 'he could already make a modest income as a card-player.' 'It would be a good idea,' Beatrice replied to him, coming closer, 'for us to set off home before you're completely ruined.' Fritz looked up at Beatrice with glowing cheeks and she smiled at him. Bertram, rising to his feet, cast a skyward glance which then fell in little sparks upon her. What's up with you all? she thought. And what's up with me? Because she suddenly realized that she was letting the lines of her body play enticingly. In search of help she fastened her eyes on the brow of her son, who, his child's face glowing and his hair unutterably untidy, was playing his final hand. He won the game and proudly received one crown and twenty haler from the architect. They prepared for the downward march, and only Frau Arbesbacher went on quietly sleeping. 'Let's leave her here,' joked the architect. But at that moment she sat up as well, rubbed her eyes and was ready for the downward climb before the rest of them.

At first their walk took them steeply downhill for a while, then almost level through young trees; at the next turning they could see the lake, which was then immediately hidden again. Beatrice, who had originally walked on ahead arm in arm with Hugo and Fritz, soon stayed behind; Leonie joined her and told her about a regatta that was going to be happening shortly. She still clearly remembered the competition seven years ago, when Ferdinand Heinhold had won second prize with the *Roxane*. The *Roxane*! Where was she now? After so many victories she led a very lonely, sluggish life in the boathouse down below. At this juncture the architect observed that sailing was just as casual as any other kind of sport these days. Leonie suggested that something mysteriously paralysing was emanating from the Welponer house, whose influence none could escape. The architect too found that the Welponers were not made for easy companionship, and his wife was of the view that the blame for this lay chiefly with the arrogance of the bank director's wife, who incidentally had really no business being like that, for all kinds of

reasons. The conversation suddenly fell silent at a bend
in the path, when the bank director was revealed, sitting
on a worm-eaten, backless bench. He rose to his feet, and
his monocle dangled on its narrow silk band over his
piqué waistcoat. He had taken the liberty, he said, of
walking towards the present company, and in the name
of his wife he invited them to a little snack which awaited
the tired hikers on the shady terrace. At the same time he
let his gloomy eyes slide from one to the other. Beatrice
noticed that they darkened noticeably on Bertram's face,
and suddenly she knew that the bank director was jealous
of the young man. She banished the thought as both
presumptuous and foolish. She wandered through life
peacefully, free of doubt, thinking in unwavering fidelity
of the only one whose voice, in memory, echoed more
resoundingly over the heights than all the voices of the
living could echo, whose gaze gleamed more brilliantly to
her than all the eyes of the living could gleam.

The bank director stayed behind with Beatrice. At first
he talked about the minor matters of the day: of newly
arrived fleeting acquaintances, of the death of the miller
who had been ninety-five, of the ugly country house that
an architect from Salzburg was building over in the Lea,
and ended up talking, as if by chance, about the time
when neither his nor the Heinolds' villa had existed, and
when the two families had spent all summer down in
the Lake Hotel. He remembered outings they had made
together on paths that were still little frequented in those
days, a boating excursion on the *Roxane* that had ended
dangerously in storms and rain, he talked of the official
opening of the Heinold villa, at which Ferdinand had
drunk two of his colleagues under the table, and finally
of Ferdinand's last role in a modern and, in the end, rather

embarrassing play, in which he had so perfectly played
the part of a twenty-year-old. What an incomparable artist
he had been, what a wonderful example of a human being!
A youthful person, you might say. A wonderful contrast
to the kind of people among whom he must sadly include
himself, who were not made to bring happiness to themselves or to others. And when Beatrice took an inquisitive
sidelong glance at him, 'My dear Frau Beatrice, I was
actually born old. Don't you know what that means? I'll
try to explain. You see, those of us who are born old,
throughout the course of our lives we drop one mask after
another, so to speak, until, at the age of eighty or so, some
of us rather later, we show our true face to the world
around us. The others, the youthful ones, and Ferdinand
was one of those,' and contrary to his custom he called
him by his first name, 'always stay young, children in fact,
and are hence required to don one mask after another, if
they don't want to be conspicuous. Or else the masks
appear from somewhere or other and slip over their faces,
and they themselves don't even know that they are wearing
them, and just have a wonderful, dark feeling that something in the sequence of their lives must be incorrect . . .
because they always feel young. Ferdinand was like that.'
Beatrice listened to the bank director excitedly but with
inner resistance. She was struck by the fact that he was
conjuring up Ferdinand's shade as if he felt the duty to
watch over her fidelity and warn and protect her against
approaching danger. He could really spare himself the
effort. What gave him the right, what gave him the
occasion to present himself as an advocate and protector
of Ferdinand's memory like this? What was it about her
that encouraged such wounding misinterpretation? If she
could laugh and joke with the cheerful ones, and if she

wore light colours as she had in the past, no objective person could see that as anything other than the modest tribute she had to pay to the universal law of living on, of living in the world. But the idea of ever feeling happiness or pleasure, of ever again belonging to a man, was one that even today she could not imagine without repulsion, without horror, and that horror, as she knew from many sleepless and lonely nights, only buried itself deeper within her when vague stirrings of longing roared through her veins and faded aimlessly away. And again she looked quickly at the bank director, now walking silently along by her side, but she was almost frightened to feel around her lips a smile that had come from the depths of her soul and which said undeniably, almost shamelessly, more clearly than any words could have done: I know you desire me, and I am pleased. In his eyes she saw a flash, like an impassioned question, but it was immediately followed by resignation and a return to melancholy. And he addressed a few indifferent and polite words to Frau Arbesbacher, who was walking only two steps ahead of them, since the little group of walkers, approaching their destination, had gradually flowed together again. Suddenly young Dr Bertram was at Beatrice's side, putting something into his posture, expression and speech as though relations between himself and Beatrice had grown more intimate during the excursion, and as though this development in his favour must also be fully apparent to her. But she remained cool and aloof, becoming more so from one step to the next. And when they had reached the garden gate of the Welponers' villa she declared to the general surprise, and also a little to her own, that she was tired and preferred to go home. They tried to change her mind. But as the bank director himself uttered only a dry word of regret, they did not push her any further. She left it open as to whether she would make it to the dinner in the Lake Hotel that had been agreed on the way, but raised no objections to Hugo joining in. 'I'll keep an eye on him,' said the architect, 'and make sure he doesn't go and get drunk.' Beatrice took her leave. A feeling of great relief came over her as she set off homewards, and she looked forward to the few undisturbed hours of which she could be certain.

At home she found a letter from Dr Teichmann and felt mild surprise, less at the fact that he had given another sign of life than because over the past little while she had forgotten him – even the fact of his existence. Only after she had shaken off the dust of the day and was sitting in a comfortable housecoat at the dressing table in her bedroom did she open the letter, about whose content she had not the slightest curiosity. It began, as usual, with communications of a social nature, because Teichmann placed particular value on Beatrice seeing him as her lawyer, and with rather tortuous humour he delivered an account of a little trial in which he had succeeded in salvaging an insignificant sum of money for Beatrice. In conclusion he mentioned, in a deliberately casual tone, that his holiday hike was also going to take him past the villa on Eichwiesenweg, and he did not wish entirely to exclude the possibility, as he wrote, of a colourful dress or even a friendly eye flashing at him through the bushes and inviting him to linger, even if only for an hour's chat in the doorway. Nor did he forget to include greetings 'to the honest architect and the esteemed lady of the manor, along with their excellent family', as he put it, and to the other acquaintances to whom he had been introduced during his three-day stay at the Lake Hotel the previous year. Beatrice found it strange that that previous year struck her as remote, as though it had fallen under a different aspect of her life, despite the fact that the outward events of her life had barely changed since that summer. There had been no shortage of gallantries on the part of the bank director and young Dr Bertram. It was just that she herself had wandered as if untouched between all their glances and words, indeed, that she had barely noticed them back then, and now only became aware of them in retrospect. The reason for that, certainly, might have been that in the city she hardly stayed in contact with all these summer acquaintances. There, since her husband's death, once the former circle of artists and theatrical enthusiasts had gradually dissolved, she had led a quiet and monotonous life. Only her mother, who lived in the old family home on the outskirts of the city, near the factory once run by her father, and some fairly distant relatives found their way to her quiet and, by now, very conventional home; and whenever Dr Teichmann came for his hour of tea and chat, it was a distraction which, as she was rather surprised to realize, she anticipated with some delight.

With a shake of her head she laid down the letter and looked into the garden, over which the early dusk of the August evening was spreading. Her contentment at being left alone had gradually ebbed away, and she wondered whether the most sensible thing might not be to go to the Welponers or, later, to the Lake Hotel. But she immediately dismissed the idea, rather ashamed that she had so completely yielded to the charms of social life, and that the wistful magic that had often surrounded her on such lonely evenings in summers past should have fled for ever. She put a thin cloth around her shoulders and went into the garden. There the gentle grief she longed for gradually enveloped her, and she knew in the depths of her soul that on those paths where she had so often walked with Ferdinand, she would never be able to stroll on another man's arm. But one thing above all was clear to her in that moment: if in those far-off days Ferdinand had beseeched her not to renounce a future happiness, he would certainly not have been thinking of matrimony with the likes of Dr Teichmann; some passionate if fleeting affair would have been more likely to win approval from Elysium. And with quiet horror she noticed that something was suddenly rising from her soul like a picture: she saw herself up on the alpine pasture in the evening dusk in the arms of Dr Bertram. But she only saw it, it was accompanied by no desire; cool and remote, like a ghost, it hung in the air and faded.

She stood at the lower end of the garden, her arms crossed over the picket fence, and looked down to where the lights of the village flickered. From the lake the song of evening boatmen came up to her through the still air with wonderful clarity. The church tower struck nine. Beatrice sighed gently, then turned around and walked slowly across the meadow to the house. On the veranda she found the usual three settings prepared. She had the maid bring her dinner, and ate it with no great pleasure and with a feeling of pointlessly muted sadness. During her meal she picked up a book; it was the reflections of the French general, which gripped her even less today than usual. The clock struck half past nine; and, as boredom crept ever more painfully into her heart, she finally resolved to leave the house and seek out the party in the Lake Hotel. She rose to her feet, put her long raw silk coat on over her housecoat and set off. When she walked past the Baroness's house by the lake, she noticed that it was in complete darkness; and it occurred to her that she hadn't seen Fortunata for several days. Had she travelled away with her captain from over the sea? But afterwards, when Beatrice turned around again, she thought she could see a shimmering light behind the closed shutters. What did it have to do with her? She paid it no attention.

On the raised terrace of the Lake Hotel, whose electric arc lamps had already been extinguished, in the dull glow of two wall lights arranged around a table, Beatrice spotted the party she had been looking for. But before she reached the table, suddenly feeling that her face was too solemnly wrinkled, she arranged it into a vacuous smile. She received a warm welcome and reached out her hand to everyone in turn, the bank director, the architect, the two wives and young Fritz Weber. Apart from them, she noticed now, there was no one else here. 'Where's Hugo?' she asked, rather unsettled. 'He's just left this minute,' answered the architect. 'Surprised you didn't meet him,' added his wife. Beatrice involuntarily glanced at Fritz, who was rolling his beer-glass back and forth with a twisted stupid-boy smile, and clearly looking past her on purpose. Then she took a seat between him and the bank director's wife and, to deaden the menacing idea that was rising up in her, she tried to talk with exaggerated animation. She was very sorry that the bank director's wife had not joined them on their lovely outing, she asked after Bertram and Leonie and talked endlessly about the fact that over dinner at home she had been reading a French memoir that was fabulously interesting. Nowadays she only ever read the memoirs and letters of great men; she no longer found pleasure in novels and the like. It turned out that everyone else present felt the same. 'Love stories are for young people,' said the architect, 'I mean for children, because to some extent we're all young people.' But Fritz too declared that he now only read scientific works, best of all descriptions of travel. While he was talking, he moved very close to Beatrice and pressed his knee to hers as if by accident, his napkin fell to the floor, he bent down to pick it up and, trembling, brushed against Beatrice's ankle. Had the boy gone insane? And he went on talking, heatedly, his eyes gleaming: once he was a doctor he would definitely go on some great expedition, maybe to Tibet or darkest Africa. His words were accompanied by a forbearing smile from the others; only the bank director, Beatrice noticed, was looking at him with grim envy. When the party rose to go home, Fritz declared that he was going to go for a lonely walk by the lake. 'Lonely?' said the architect. 'We can choose to believe that or not.' But Fritz replied that such nocturnal summer walks were his particular passion; only recently had he come home at about one o'clock in the morning, with Hugo, who also liked to go on night-time outings. And when he felt Beatrice's uneasily questioning eyes upon him, he added, 'It's highly possible that I will meet Hugo somewhere on the shore, if he hasn't rowed out, which also sometimes happens.' 'This is all news to me,' said Beatrice with a shake of her head. 'Yes, these summer nights,' sighed the architect. 'You can talk,' remarked his wife mysteriously. Frau Welponer, who walked ahead of the others down the terrace steps, stopped for a moment, looked up questioningly into the sky, and then lowered her head in a strangely hopeless way. The bank director remained silent. But in his silence there was hatred for summer nights, youth and happiness.

Hardly had they all reached the shore when Fritz dashed away as if joking, and disappeared into the darkness. Beatrice was accompanied home by the two couples. They all toiled slowly up the steep path. Why did Fritz run off so suddenly? Has he ever rowed out on to the lake with Hugo at night? Have they made a pact? Does Fritz know where Hugo is at this moment? Does he know? And she came to a stop, because she felt as though her heart had suddenly stopped beating. As if I myself didn't know where Hugo was. As if I hadn't known for days! 'It would be so good,' the architect said, 'if they'd put a chairlift up here.' He had offered his wife his arm, something, as far as Beatrice could recall, he never normally tended to do. The bank director and his wife walked side by side at an even pace, bowed and silent. By the time Beatrice reached her door, she knew Fritz had run off down below. He had wanted to avoid disappearing into the villa with her alone at night in full view of the others. And she felt gratitude for the young man's gallant cleverness. The bank director kissed Beatrice's hand. Whatever may befall you, his silence tremulously said, I will understand, and you will have a friend in me. – Leave me alone, replied Beatrice just as silently. The two couples parted. The bank director and his wife disappeared with curious haste into the darkness where forest, mountain and sky merged. The Arbesbachers took the path towards the other side, where the landscape was more open and the star-blue night stretched over gentle hills.

When the door had closed behind her, Beatrice thought: should I take a look in Hugo's room? What for? I know he isn't at home. I know he's in the place where the light was shimmering behind the closed shutters earlier on. And it occurred to her that on her way home just now she had walked past that house again, and that she had seen it in darkness, like others nearby. Yet she no longer doubted that her son had been in the villa as she was walking past it, thoughtlessly and yet with a sense of foreboding. And she also knew that she was to blame. She, yes, she alone: because she had allowed it to happen. On that visit to Fortunata she had thought she had fulfilled all her maternal duties all at once, from then on she had let things take their course – out of inertia, out of tiredness, out of cowardice, she had not wanted to see anything, know anything, think anything. Hugo was with Fortunata at that moment, and not for the first time. An image arose in her that made her shudder, and she hid her face in her hands as if by doing so she could frighten it away. She was engulfed by grief as though she had just said goodbye to something that could never return. Gone was the time when Hugo had been a child, her child. Now he was a young man, someone who lived his own life, about which he could no longer tell his mother anything. Never again will she be able to stroke his cheeks, his hair, never again kiss his sweet child's lips as once she did. Only now, now that she had lost him too, was she truly alone.

She sat on the bed and slowly began to undress. How long will he stay out? Probably the whole night. And at dawn, very quietly, so as not to wake his mother, he will creep down the corridor to his room. How often might it have happened already? How many nights has he spent with her? Many? No – not many. He even spent a few days hiking across country. Yes, if he was telling the truth! But he doesn't tell the truth any more. He hasn't done so for ages. In the winter he plays billiards in suburban coffee-houses, and who knows where he spends the rest of his time? And all of a sudden an idea sent the blood rushing faster through her veins: was he Fortunata's lover even *then*? On the day when she paid her ridiculous visit to the villa by the lake? And the Baroness was just acting out a pitiful little comedy, and then, with Hugo, heart to heart with Hugo, she had mocked her and laughed at her? Yes . . . that too was possible. Because what did she now know about her boy, who had become a man in the arms of a prostitute? Nothing . . . nothing.

She leaned against the balustrade of the open window and looked into the garden and beyond it to the dark mountain peaks on the opposite shore. There, sharply outlined, loomed that one that not even Dr Bertram dared to climb. Why hadn't he been down in the Lake Hotel? If he'd guessed that she was coming, he'd certainly have been there. Wasn't it strange that they still desired her, when she was already the mother of a son who spent his nights with a lover? Why strange? She was as young as, perhaps younger than, that Fortunata. And all of a sudden, with agonizing clarity and yet with painful pleasure, she could feel the outlines of her body beneath her thin clothing. A sound outside in the corridor made her jump. She knew that was Fritz coming home. Where had he been running about until now? Was he having a little affair of his own here in the village? She smiled mournfully. Not him. He was even a little in love with her. No wonder, really. She was exactly the right age to appeal to such a green boy. He had probably wanted to cool his passion in the night air; and she felt a little sorry for him, when the sky hung so heavy and misty over the lake. And suddenly she remembered one such summer night from a time she had long ago forgotten, when her husband had, despite her resistance, taken her from the gentle mystery of the marriage bed into the garden and, pressed close to her, caressed her wildly in the night-black shade of the trees. She also thought of the cool morning when a thousand birds' voices had woken her to a sweet and heavy sadness, and she shivered. Where had it all gone? Wasn't it as if the garden below her had preserved the memory of those nights better than she had herself? Might it not in some miraculous way reveal that memory to those who knew how to listen to silence? And she felt as though that night itself was in the garden, ghostly and mysterious, as if every house, every garden had a night of its own, one that was quite different, more profound and more intimate than the insensate blue darkness that stretched out into the unknown far above the sleeping world. And the night that belonged to her was now filled with secrets and dreams beyond the window, staring into her face with their blind eyes. Spontaneously, her hands stretched out as if in self-defence, she walked back into the room, then turned away, let her shoulders fall, stepped to the mirror and began to loosen her hair. It must be past midnight. She was at once tired and wide awake. What was the use of all thought, all memory, all dreaming, what use all fear and hope? Hope? What hope still existed for her? Again she walked to the window and carefully closed the shutters. The light is shining into the night, into my night, she thought fleetingly. She locked the door leading on to the corridor, then, according to careful old custom, she opened the door to the little drawing-room to glance inside. She gave a start of terror. In the semi-darkness, standing upright in the middle of the room, she could make out a male form. 'Who is it?' she cried. The form moved towards her. Beatrice recognized Fritz. 'What are you thinking of?' she said. But he dashed towards her and gripped both her hands. Beatrice pulled them away: 'You aren't thinking straight.' 'Forgive me, *gnädige Frau*,' he whispered, 'but I . . . I don't know what to do.' 'It's very simple,' answered Beatrice, 'go to bed.' He shook his head. 'Go now, go on,' she said, went back to her room and was about to close the door behind her. Then she felt someone touching her gently and rather clumsily on the neck. She gave a start, turned around automatically and reached out an arm as though to push Fritz away, but he grasped her hand and pressed it to his lips. 'But Fritz,' she said, more gently than she had intended. – 'I'm going insane,' he whispered. She smiled. 'I think you are already.' – 'I would have kept watch here all night,' he continued in a whisper, 'I didn't guess that you would open that door. I just wanted to be here, *gnädige Frau*, here near you.' – 'But now go right back to your room. Will you do that? Or else you'll really make me angry.' – He had brought both her hands to his lips. 'I beg you, *gnädige Frau*.' – 'Don't do anything stupid, Fritz! That's enough! Let go of my hands. That's right. And now go.' He had dropped her hands and she felt the warm breath of his mouth around her cheeks. 'I'm going mad. I've been in this room here for a while now.' – 'What?' – 'Yes, half the night, almost until daybreak. I can't do anything about it. I want to be near you.' – 'Don't talk such nonsense.' He went on stammering, 'I beg you, *gnädige* Frau Beatrice – Beatrice – Beatrice.' – 'That's quite enough, now. You really are – what are you thinking of? Shall I call someone? For God's sake! Just think! Hugo!' 'Hugo isn't at home. No one can hear us.' For a moment a burning pain shot through her again. Then she suddenly realized, with shame and horror, that she was glad Hugo was far away. She felt Fritz's warm lips on hers, and within her there arose a longing that she never, even in times long past, thought she would ever feel again. Who can think ill of me? she thought. To whom am I accountable? And with yearning arms she drew the ardent boy to her.

Chapter Three

When Beatrice stepped from the darkness of the forest shade and out beneath the open sky, the gravel path stretched before her, burning and brilliant white, and she almost regretted leaving the Welponers' villa so early in the afternoon. But since the lady of the house had disappeared for her usual nap straight after lunch, and their son and daughter had disappeared without any further explanation, Beatrice would have had to stay on her own with the bank director, something which, after the experiences of the past few days, she wished to avoid at all costs. His attempts to find favour with her had grown all too obvious, indeed certain hints from him led Beatrice to suspect that he would be prepared to leave his wife and children for her sake; perhaps even that a relationship with Beatrice, more than anyone else, would provide him with the desired release from domestic circumstances that had grown intolerable. Because, with her eye for human relations which had lately grown almost painfully sharp, Beatrice had discerned that that marriage was under great strain, and that at some unexpected moment, even without any external cause, it could collapse. She had often been struck by the excessive caution with which the couple tended to address one another, as though the simmering rage that seemed to lurk in the hard folds around the mouths of the ageing pair might at any moment discharge into angry and irreparable words; but only that incredible thing, the thing that she still didn't believe, which Fritz had told her in the night just past, the rumour of an affair that was said to have occurred between the bank director's wife and Beatrice's late husband, made her contemplate the causes of such a serious breakdown with genuine sympathy. And although over lunch, with harmless and indifferent small talk moving back and forth across the table, the rumour had still struck her as completely nonsensical, now that she was walking home along the path through the meadow, through the shimmering summer air from whose sweltering heat all living things seemed to have fled for the shade of closed rooms, Fritz's indelicate suggestions began to affect her in a vivid and agonizing way. Why, she wondered, did he speak of it, and why only that night? Had it been revenge because, when he was supposed to go to his parents' house in Bad Ischl in the morning, she had asked him, half jokingly, to stay there rather than come back, as he planned, that evening? Had he jealously come to suspect that for all his youthful charms he meant no more to her than a fresh and handsome boy who could simply be sent home once the game was over? Or had he only yielded to his tendency to indiscreet gossip for which she had sometimes had occasion to rebuke him, as just recently, for example, when he had wanted to tell her more about Hugo's introduction to Fortunata? Or was the conversation between Fritz's parents, upon which he claimed lately to have eavesdropped, merely an invention of his imaginative mind, just as his visit to the dissecting room, which he had described on the day of his arrival, had recently turned out to be idle boasting? But, even allowing that he was reporting his parents' conversation in good faith, might he not have misunderstood or misinterpreted it? This last suspicion was made all the more plausible since not the quietest word of the rumour had reached Beatrice.

Immersed in these reflections, Beatrice had reached her villa. Since Hugo had supposedly gone on an outing and it was the maid's day off, Beatrice found herself alone at home. She undressed in her bedroom and, yielding to an oppressive fatigue that often overcame her during these afternoons, she stretched out on her bed. Consciously enjoying the solitude, the silence, the very muted light, she lay there for a while with her eyes open. In the crooked dressing table mirror opposite her there appeared the life-size head-and-shoulders portrait of her late husband which hung over her bed. But all that she could clearly see was a dull red patch that she knew represented the carnation in his buttonhole. For a while immediately after Ferdinand's death that painting had continued to have a strange life of its own. She had seen it smiling or looking grim, she had seen it cheerful and melancholy; sometimes, indeed, it was as though her husband's painted features mysteriously expressed indifference or despair at his own death. Over the years, certainly, the portrait had grown mute and closed; it remained a painted canvas and nothing more. But today, at this moment, it seemed to want to come alive again. And although Beatrice could not see it clearly in the mirror, it was as though it was sending a mocking gaze upon her, and memories arose in her which, however harmless or even cheerful they might hitherto have been, pushed into her mind's eye with new and scornful gestures. And instead of the one upon whom her suspicion had fallen, a whole series of women drew past her, some of them forgotten apart from their facial features, maybe all of whom, it suddenly occurred to her, had been Ferdinand's lovers – fans collecting autographs and photographs, young artists who had studied with him, society ladies whose salons he and Beatrice had frequented, colleagues who had fallen into his arms on stage as wives, brides, fallen women. And she wondered whether it might not have been his own guilt which, while it did not particularly oppress him, none the less filled him with such seemingly wise tolerance of the infidelity that Beatrice might one day commit against his memory. And all of a sudden, as though he had cast aside the mask which had grown useless and uncomfortable, which he had worn long enough alive and dead, he appeared before her mind's eye with the red carnation in his buttonhole like a foppish ham actor for whom she had been nothing more than an efficient housewife, the mother of his son, the kind of woman one would sometimes embrace from time to time when, on tepid summer nights, the dull enchantment of togetherness would have it so. And like his picture, all of a sudden his voice too was incomprehensibly changed. It no longer rang out with the noble timbre which, in her memory, still sounded more magnificent than the voice of anyone alive; it sounded empty, affected and false. But suddenly, at once frightened and relieved, she became aware that it was not really his voice that echoed in her soul, but that of another, of one who had lately dared, had dared here in her house, to parody the body, tone and gestures of her late husband.

She sat up in bed, rested her arm on the pillow and stared with horror into the gloom of the bedroom. Only now, in the utter quiet of that time of night, did the event in all its monstrosity appear before her mind's eye. It had been a week ago, on a Sunday like today, she had been sitting in the garden in the company of her son and – she thought the word with her lips pressed tight – her lover, when all of a sudden a young man had appeared, tall, dark haired, with flashing eyes, dressed like a tourist, with a green, yellow and red tie – someone she didn't recognize before the delighted welcome he received from the two other young people made her realize that Rudi Beratoner was standing before her, the Rudi who had visited Hugo a few times the past winter to borrow books from him, and of whom she knew that he was one of the two who, by Hugo's account, had made a merry spring night of it in the Prater with foolish young females. Today he was coming straight from Ischl, where he had sought Fritz in vain at the house of his parents, and of course he had been kept there for lunch. He seemed funny, noisy, especially tireless in the recounting of hunting tales and all kinds of anecdotes, and his two younger schoolmates, who seemed almost boyish in comparison to his precocity, looked up to him in admiration. He also showed a head for drink beyond his years. Since his friends did not wish to take second place to him, and even Beatrice allowed herself to be tempted into drinking more than usual, the mood soon grew more relaxed than was usual in this house. Beatrice, who was agreeably touched by, even grateful for, her guest's respectful behaviour towards her despite all the merriment, felt, as she sometimes did during this time, that all the things that had lately happened to her, whose reality she could not doubt, seemed either a dream or something that could be remedied. At one moment, as often before, she had her arm draped around Hugo's shoulders and was playing with her fingers in his hair, but at the same time she looked with tender temptation into Fritz's eyes, and felt strangely moved about herself and the world. Later she noticed that Fritz was whispering insistently to Rudi Beratoner and seemed to be telling him something urgent. She asked, as if joking, what dangerous matters the young gentlemen had to whisper about; Beratoner didn't want to say anything, but Fritz declared there was no reason why they shouldn't speak of it; it was generally known that Rudi was excellent at imitating actors, not only the living but also the – and here he stopped. But Beatrice, deeply excited and already slightly intoxicated, turned quickly to Rudi Beratoner, and asked in a rather hoarse voice, 'So can you imitate Ferdinand Heinold?' She uttered the famous name as though it belonged to a stranger. Beratoner wouldn't hear of it. He didn't know what Fritz was talking about, he had enjoyed such pranks in the past, but not for ages; and of course he no longer had an ear for voices he hadn't heard for years, and if he had to do anything of the kind he would rather sing some couplet in the manner of a popular comedian. But Beatrice wouldn't accept his excuse. She felt only the wish not to let the opportunity pass. She trembled with the desire to hear the beloved voice again, or at least a reflection of it. That there might be something vicious in that desire barely occurred to her in the haze of the moment. Finally Beratoner yielded. And with pounding heart Beatrice heard first Hamlet's soliloquy ringing out through the clear summer air in Ferdinand's heroic intonation, then lines from Tasso, then some long-forgotten words from some long-forgotten play; heard the roaring and melting away of that voice she had loved, and drank it in intensely like a miracle with her eyes closed, until suddenly, and it was still Ferdinand's voice, but now in his familiar everyday tone, close by her ear, she heard the words, 'Hallo, Beatrice!' At this, deeply shocked, she opened her eyes, saw close before her a cheekily embarrassed face, around its lips a fading tension that eerily recalled Ferdinand's smile, met a crazed expression in Hugo's eyes, a stupid and sad grin around Fritz's mouth and heard herself, as if from a long way off, addressing a polite word of thanks to the excellent impressionist. The silence that followed was dark and oppressive; none of them could bear it for long, and soon indifferently cheerful words of summer weather and the joys of excursions floated back and forth. But Beatrice soon rose to her feet and withdrew to her room, where she dropped into her armchair and then fell into a sleep from which she emerged again after barely an hour, but as if from the depths of night. Later, when she stepped into the garden in the cool of evening, the young people had gone, soon returning without Rudi Beratoner, about whom, clearly deliberately, they said nothing more; and it was a quiet consolation for Beatrice, the way her son and her lover, with their particularly careful and delicate behaviour, tried to erase the painful impression of that afternoon.

And now, as Beatrice tried to remember her husband's real voice in the dusky silence of a lonely hour, she couldn't. Time and again, it was the voice of that unwelcome guest that echoed within her; and more deeply than before she became aware how great an abuse she had committed against the dead man, worse than anything he could have done to her even in his lifetime; more cowardly and impossible to atone for than infidelity and betrayal. He was decaying in the dark depths of the earth, and his widow let stupid boys make fun of him, the wonderful man she had loved, she alone, despite everything that had happened, just as she had loved no one else but him and would love no one else. Only now did she know it, now that she had a lover. A lover! Oh, if only he never returned, the one who had been her lover! – If only he was out of her sight for ever and out of her blood, and she was living alone again with her Hugo in the sweet summer peace of her villa, as before. As before? And if Fritz is no longer there, will she have her son back? Has she not the right to expect it? Has she paid him any attention recently? Had she not rather been happy that he was going his own way? And it occurred to her that lately, on a walk with the Arbesbachers, she had glimpsed her son hardly a hundred paces away at the edge of the forest, in the company of Fortunata, Wilhelmine Fallehn and a male stranger; and she – she had hardly been ashamed, she had just gone on talking insistently to her companions, so that they didn't notice Hugo. And on the evening of the same day, yesterday – yes, of course, it was only yesterday, how incomprehensible was the passing of time! – she had met Fräulein Fallehn and that stranger, who, with his black gleaming hair, his flashing white teeth, his moustache trimmed in the English fashion, his raw silk suit and his bright red silk shirt, looked to her like a circus rider, a confidence trickster or a Mexican millionaire. As Wilhelmine lowered her head in greeting, with her immovably profound air of gravity, he too had doffed his straw hat, flashed his teeth and studied Beatrice with an impudently laughing smile that made her blush even to remember it. What a pair they were! She thought them capable of all manner of crime and vice. And those were Fortunata's friends, those were the people with whom her son went walking now, whose company he kept. Beatrice threw her hands to her face, groaned quietly and whispered to herself: away, away away! She uttered the word without really knowing what place she had in mind. Only gradually did she feel its entire meaning, and sense that it might contain salvation for herself and Hugo. Yes, they had to go away, both of them, mother and son, and as quickly as possible. She had to take him with her – or else he had to take her. They both had to leave the town before something irreparable happened, before the mother's reputation was destroyed, before the son's youth was completely corrupted, before fate had closed over them both. There was still time. No one knew of her own experience, or she would somehow have been able to tell, at least from the behaviour of the architect. And certainly nothing was yet known of her son's affair. And if it was, no one would hold it against the inexperienced boy: and neither could anyone reproach the mother, hitherto so carefree, as long as she took flight with her son as if she had only just discovered the truth. So it wasn't too late. The problem lay elsewhere: in persuading her son to leave so suddenly. Beatrice had no idea of the extent of the Baroness's power over Hugo's heart and senses. She knew nothing, nothing about him, since she had had her own affairs to deal with. But, clever as he was, he could not be blind to the fact that his affair with Fortunata would not last for ever, and so he would be able to understand that a few days more or less were of little importance. And in her mind she spoke to him: we're not going back to Vienna straight away! Oh, there's no question of that, my boy. We'll head south, shall we? We've been planning that for ages. To Venice, to Florence, to Rome. Just think, you'll be able to see Caesar's imperial palaces! And St Peter's! . . . Hugo! We're setting off tomorrow. Just you and me. A trip like that one we took two years ago this spring. Do you remember? We took the coach via

Mürzsteg to Mariazell. Wasn't that lovely? And it'll be even lovelier this time. And if it's a bit hard for you at first, goodness, I know, I'm not asking you and you don't have to say a word to me. But when you see so many new and lovely things, you'll forget. You'll forget very quickly. Much more quickly than you can guess. – And what about you, mother? – The question came from the very depths of her, in Hugo's voice. She gave a start. And she quickly took her hands from her eyes, as if to check that she was alone. Yes, she was. Quite alone in the house, in the gloom of the bedroom; outside the summer day breathed heavy and sultry, no one could disturb her. She had peace and time to consider what to say to her son. And that was certain: she didn't need to fear a reply like the one her senses had conjured for her. 'And what about you, mother?' He couldn't ask her that. Because he didn't know anything, he couldn't know anything. And he will never know anything. Even if a dark rumour should reach his ear, he won't believe it. He'll never believe anything like that of his mother. She can be reassured about that. And she sees herself strolling with him in some imaginary landscape probably remembered from a painting, on a greyish-yellow road – and in the distance, in the sky, hovers a city with many towers. And then again they are walking around in a big square under arcades, strangers come towards her and look at them, her and her son. They look at them with such curiosity, with an impudent, flashing smile, and think: oh, she's brought a nice boy on her travels with her. She could be his mother. What? People take them for a couple? Well, and why not. They can't know that the boy is her son; and they probably decide that she's one of those over-ripe women with a taste for young blood. And there they are now, the two of them, walking around in a strange city, among people they don't know, and he is thinking of his dearest love with the Pierrot face and she of her sweet fair boy. She groans out loud. She wrings her hands. Where to now? Where to? Just now the pet name had passed her lips, the name with which she had tenderly held him to her bosom last night. The one to whom she will now say farewell for ever, and whom she will never, never see again. Although of course she will, once more, today, when he comes back. Or tomorrow morning. But tonight her door will be closed for ever. It is over for ever. And she will tell him by way of farewell that she loved him very much, more than anyone ever will, surely, ever again. And filled with this proud emotion he will become all the more deeply aware of his chivalrous duty to maintain eternal silence. And he will understand that they must part, and he will kiss her hand again and he will go. He will go. And what then? What then? And she feels herself lying there with her lips half opened, her arms spread, her body trembling, and she knows: if he walked through the door at that moment, young and full of yearning, she could not resist him, and would be his once again with all the fervour that has now awoken within her like something forgotten for years, like something she has never even known. And now she also knows, with both bliss and agony, that the youth to whom she gave herself will not have been her last lover. But already an ardent curiosity is welling up in her: who will the next one be? Dr Bertram? One evening comes into her memory – was it three days ago, a week? – she doesn't know, time stretches out and retracts, the hours merge into one another and cease to mean anything – it had been in the park at the Welponers', where, in a dark avenue, Bertram had suddenly pulled her to him, wrapped his arms around her and kissed her. And although she had pushed him violently from her, what could it have meant to him, when he must have felt the lasting pressure of her lips, so accustomed to kissing? That was why he had immediately become so calm and modest, as though he knew precisely what he was dealing with, and his expression read: winter belongs to me, lovely woman. We reached an agreement long ago. We both know that death is a bitter thing and virtue but an empty word and that one shouldn't miss a thing. But it wasn't Bertram who was talking to her. All of a sudden, while she lay there with her eyes closed, another face had pushed beneath Bertram's, that of the circus rider or confidence trickster or Mexican who had recently stared at her so cheekily, just as Bertram and all kinds of other people did. They all had the same expression, all of them, and that expression always said and desired and knew the same thing; and if one got involved with one of them, one was lost. They took the women they happened to fancy at the time, and then discarded them again . . . Yes – if one allowed oneself to be taken and discarded. But she wasn't one of those. No, things hadn't yet gone that far. Fleeting affairs were not for her. If she had been born to such things, how could she have taken that business with Fritz so badly? And if she is now suffering, regretting, tormenting herself, it is only because what she has done is so completely against her nature. She doesn't really understand how it could all have happened. And it isn't to be explained except by the fact that in those unbearable sultry summer days something like an illness afflicted her, making her defenceless and confused. And just as the illness came, so it will go again. Soon, soon. She can feel it in her every pulse, her senses, throughout her whole body, that she isn't the same person as she was. She can barely collect her thoughts. They rush feverishly through her brain. She doesn't know what she wants, what she desires, what she regrets, she barely knows if she is happy or unhappy. It must be an illness. With some women a state like that can last for ages and not go away: Fortunata might be one of those women, and that alabaster-pale Fräulein Fallehn. And with others it comes upon them all of a sudden or insinuates itself and soon goes away again. And that is her case. Quite certainly. How did she live all those years since Ferdinand went away? Modest as a young girl, free of desire. Only this summer has it come upon her. Might there be something in the air this year? The women all look different; so do the girls, they have brighter, more insolent eyes, and their gestures are careless, enticing and seductive. You hear all sorts of things! What sort of story was that about the young doctor's wife who went out on to the lake at night with a boatman and, they said, only came home again the next morning? And the two young girls who lay naked over there on the meadow just as the little steamship was passing and suddenly, before anyone could recognize them, disappeared into the woods? That's it, it's in the air this year. The sun has a special power, and the waves of the lake lap more sweetly around one's limbs than ever. And when the mysterious spell is broken, she too will be as she was, she will have slipped through the ardent adventure of these days and nights as through a dream that will soon be forgotten. And when she feels it approaching again, as once again she has felt it approaching long before it arrives, when the longing in her blood seems to surge menacingly – this time she will be able to choose a better and a purer kind of escape, like other women in the same situation, embark upon a second marriage. But now a scornful smile, one that seemed almost surprised at itself, rose to her lips. She thought of someone who had recently been there, and who she believed harboured the most honest intentions: the lawyer Dr Teichmann. She saw him before her in his spanking brand new green and yellow speckled tourist's suit with his tartan tie, wearing his green hat with its chamois tuft at a rakish angle, in brief in a get-up clearly designed to prove to her that he knew how to look very businesslike, even if, as a serious man, he placed no value on such externals under ordinary circumstances. Then she saw him, sitting over lunch on the veranda between her son and her lover, addressing now one, now the other, with the self-importance of a headmaster – and saw him in all his ridiculous innocence, which had moved her, in a cheeky mood, to press Fritz's hands tenderly under the table. The same evening he had set off again, to meet friends in Bozen; and although Beatrice had not invited him to stay, he seemed very light-hearted and hopeful as he set off, because in her arrogant mood that summer day she had given him too no shortage of encouraging and promising glances. Now she regretted that as well, like so much else, and she felt all the more uncertain as she anticipated her next discussion with Teichmann, becoming painfully aware of the gradual waning of her willpower in the deep fatigue of the evening. With similar shame, she recalled how defenceless she had sometimes felt during her last conversations with Herr Welponer; and she felt that, faced with a choice, she could more easily imagine herself as the bank director wife, indeed she had to admit that the idea was not without a certain charm. Today she even felt as if she had always been interested in him; and everything the architect had told her lately about the bank director's grandiose speculations and battles, in which he had triumphed over ministers and members of the court, was designed to arouse Beatrice's curiosity and admiration. And, by the by, Teichmann had referred to him in conversation as a genius, and likened him, in the boldness of his enterprises, which, for Teichmann, were always the supreme achievement, to a fearless cavalry general. So Beatrice could probably be a little flattered that this man, of all men, seemed to desire her, quite apart from the satisfaction she could derive from taking the husband of a woman who had robbed her of her own. Robbed me of my own? she asked herself with confused surprise. What is happening to me? Where am I going? Can I believe this? It can't be true. Anything but that. I would surely have noticed something. Noticed something? Why? Was Ferdinand not an actor, and a great one at that? Why couldn't it have happened without my noticing? I was so trusting, it can't have been hard to deceive me. Not hard . . . But that doesn't mean it must have happened. Fritz is a loudmouth, a liar, and the rumours are stupid lies too. And if it did happen, well, it was a long time ago. And Ferdinand is dead. And his lover then is an old woman now. Why should I concern myself with all the things that happened in the past? What is going on now between the bank director and myself is something entirely new that has nothing to do with anything that happened in the past. Really, she went on thinking, it wouldn't be so terrible to move in there one day, into the royal villa with the big park. What wealth, what elegance! And what wonderful prospects for Hugo's future! . . . Of course, he was not a young man. And that was relevant to some extent, particularly if one was as spoilt as she had been recently. Yes, in the course of the summer, in the course of the past few weeks, he had seemed to age unusually quickly. Might his love for her be partly to blame? Well, and what if it was? There are younger women as well, someone will deceive him; it's obviously his fate. She laughed briefly, it sounded ugly and mean, and she gave a start, as if waking from a barren dream. Where am I? Where am I? She stretched her hands skywards. How much deeper will you let me sink! Is there no resting place? What is it that makes me so wretched, so pitiful? What makes me clutch at random into the void, making me no better than Fortunata and all the women of that kind? And suddenly, her heartbeat failing, she knew what was making her miserable: the ground on which she had walked in safety for years was rocking, and the sky above her was darkening: the only man she had loved, her Ferdinand, had been a liar. Yes . . . she knew it now. His whole life with her had been nothing but deception and hypocrisy; he had betrayed her with Frau Welponer and with other women, with actresses and countesses and prostitutes. And if, on sultry nights, the dull enchantment of togetherness had driven him into Beatrice's arms, of all the lies that had been the worst and the lowest, because she knew that at her breast he had been thinking with lubricious malice of the others, all the others. But how did she know that all of a sudden? Because she had been no different, no better than he! Had it been Ferdinand she had held in her arms, the actor with the red carnation, who, often enough, hadn't come home from the pub until three in the morning, stinking of wine? Who had droned on, dull-eyed, about vacuous and smutty subjects? Who, as a young man, had denied an ageing widow his elegant passions and, in merry company, read out tender little notes sent to his dressing-room by infatuated fools? No, him she had never loved. She would have run away from him in the first month of her marriage. The one she loved had not been Ferdinand Heinold: it had been Hamlet, and Cyrano and King Richard and this one and that one, heroes and criminals, victors and those destined for death, the blessed and the damned. And also the strangely luminous one, who had once, on an overcast summer night, enticed her from the silent gloom of the marital chamber and into the garden with him to enjoy unimaginable ecstasies, that hadn't been Ferdinand, but some mysteriously powerful spirit from the mountains, whose part he was acting unawares – had to act because without a mask he couldn't have lived, because he would have been horrified to glimpse his true face reflected in her eye. Like that, she had always deceived him, just as he had deceived her – she had always, a lost woman from the very outset, led a life of wild and imaginary pleasure; but no one could ever have suspected it, not even she herself. – But now it had been made obvious. She was meant to slide ever deeper, and one day, who knows how soon, it will be clear to the whole world that the whole of her bourgeois respectability was a lie, that she is no better than Fortunata, Wilhelmine Fallehn and all the others she has despised until now. And her son too will know; and if he doesn't believe the story about Fritz, he will believe, have to believe a story to come; and suddenly she sees him before her, eyes wide open with pain, arms stretched out before him in self-defence; and as she tries to approach him, he turns away from her in horror and dashes off with the flying steps of dreams. And she groans out loud, suddenly wide awake. Lose Hugo! Anything – anything but that. Sooner die than have no son. Die, yes. Because then she would have him back. Then he comes to his mother's grave and kneels down and adorns it with flowers and folds his hands and prays for her. At this thought emotion creeps, sweet and repellent, deceptively peaceful, into her soul. But deep within her there is a whisper: Can I rest? All those things still to be done ... So much ... so much ...

And in the gloomy silence that surrounded her she sensed that outside, the world, the people and the country-side must have woken from their summer afternoon slumber. All kinds of distant sounds, indefinite and confused, reached her through the closed shutters. And she knew that the people were already strolling along the paths, rowing boats, playing tennis and drinking coffee on the hotel terrace; indeed, in her still half-dreaming state she saw a jolly throng of summer people, small as toys but floating up and down before her, colourful and distinct. The pocket-watch on her bedside table ticked loudly, almost urgently, in her ear. Beatrice suddenly felt the need to know what time it was, but she didn't yet have the strength to turn her head or even to switch on the light. Some new, closer sound, clearly from the garden, had gradually reached her ear. What could it be? People's voices, without a doubt. So close? Voices in the garden? Hugo and Fritz? How could the two of them be back already? Well, evening is falling, and Fritz's yearning will have driven him back so early. But Hugo? She hadn't dared hope that he would be home from his so-called trip before midnight. But who opened the door to them? Hadn't she bolted it? And the maid can't be back yet. They must have rung first and she ignored it in her sleep. Then they'll have climbed over the fence again, and of course they can't suspect that the lady of the house is at home. Now one of them is laughing outside. What sort of laugh is that? It isn't Hugo's laugh. But Fritz doesn't laugh like that either. Now the other one's laughing. That isn't Hugo. He's talking. That isn't Hugo's voice either. So is Fritz in the garden with someone else? Now they're very close. They seem to have sat down outside on the bench, the white one under the window. And now she hears Fritz calling the other one by name. Rudi. So he's sitting with him under her window. Well, that's hardly such a surprise. It had recently been agreed in her presence that Rudi Beratoner should soon come over to see them again. Perhaps he'd turned up earlier, found nobody there and then, at the station or somewhere, bumped into Fritz, driven back from Ischl so early by his love. At least there was no reason to rack her brains over it. They were there now, the two young gentlemen, sitting in the garden on the white bench under the window of the next room. But now it was time to get up, get dressed and go out into the garden. Why? Did she really have to go into the garden? Did she have a special desire to see Fritz again or did she just feel like saying hello to the shameless young man who had recently impersonated her late husband's voice and gestures with such mocking accuracy? But in the end her only option was to say good evening to the young people. She couldn't stay so quiet for any length of time while the two of them were chattering about whatever took their fancy. One could assume that it was not a particularly clean conversation. Well, that had nothing to do with her. Let them say what they wished.

Beatrice had got up and was sitting on the edge of the bed. Then, for the first time, she heard a word with complete clarity, her son's name. Of course they were talking about Hugo; and what they were saying was not hard to guess. Now they were laughing again. But the words were impossible to make out. Close to the window she would have been able to follow the conversation, but perhaps it was better not to. One could have unpleasant surprises. The most sensible thing in the end was to make oneself ready as quickly as possible and go into the garden. But Beatrice first felt compelled to creep very quietly over to the closed shutters. She peered out through a narrow crack and could see nothing but a strip of green; then, through another, a strip of blue sky. But now she would be better able to hear what was being said out there on the bench. Again all she could hear was her Hugo's name. Everything else sounded as whispered and faint as if they had realized they might be heard. Beatrice put her ear to the crack and smiled with a sigh of relief. They were talking about school. She heard very clearly: 'The creep would really have liked to fail him.' And then: 'A scoundrel.' She crept back, quickly wrapped herself in a comfortable housecoat: then, in the grip of irrepressible curiosity, she slipped back to the window. And now she discovered that they had stopped talking about school. 'You say she's a baroness?' That was Rudi Beratoner's voice. And now . . . goodness, that was an ugly word. 'He was with her all day, and today –' Oh, that was Fritz's voice. She spontaneously covered her ears, moved away from the window and resolved to hurry into the garden straight away. But before she had reached the door she was compelled back to the window, she knelt down, put her ear to the crack and listened, eyes wide and cheeks aflame.

Rudi Beratoner was telling a story, sometimes his voice fell to a whisper, but from the individual words that Beatrice could hear it gradually became clear what he was discussing. Rudi was talking about a love affair; Beatrice could hear pet names in French, delivered in a thin and sickly voice. So he was clearly copying the manner of that person's speech. He was excellent at that. Who's sleeping in the next room? His sister. Ah, it's the governess . . . And on . . . on . . . What is the arrangement? When his sister is asleep, the governess comes to his room. And then, and then . . . ? Beatrice doesn't want to hear, but she goes on listening with mounting curiosity. What words! What a tone! So that's how these boys talk about their lovers! No, no, not all of them and not about all of their lovers. What kind of woman must that be! She probably deserved to be talked about in that way and no other. Why did she deserve it? What crime had she committed, after all? And it only became repellent if it was talked about. When Rudi Beratoner was holding her in his arms he was sure to be tender, he would have words of love for her – as they all do in such moments. If only she could have seen Fritz's face. Oh, she could imagine it. His cheeks were burning and his eyes were glowing. Now it grew very quiet for a while. The tale was obviously over. And suddenly she heard Fritz's voice. He's asking a question. What? Must you really know everything in such detail? A dull feeling of jealousy stirs in Beatrice. What – you're going to answer that as well? Yes, Rudi Beratoner is talking. At least talk a bit louder, then. I want to hear what you're saying, you rogue, who insulted my husband in the grave and are now humiliating and slandering your lover. Louder! Oh, God, it was loud enough. He wasn't telling a story any more. He was asking a question. He wanted to know whether Fritz had, here in the town – yes, you scoundrel, just wallow in your vulgarities. It won't do you any good. You won't learn anything. Fritz is almost only a boy, but he's more chivalrous than you. He knows what he owes a respectable woman who has bestowed her favours upon him. Isn't that right, Fritz, my sweet Fritz, you won't say anything? What was it that fixed her to the floor so that she couldn't stand up, dash out and put a stop to the scandalous conversation? But what good would it have done? Rudi Beratoner wasn't the man to give up so easily. If he doesn't get his answer today, right now, he'll repeat the question an hour later. The best thing is to stay here and go on listening, at least then you know what's going on. Why so quiet, Fritz? Say something. Why shouldn't you boast of your good fortune? A respectable woman like me . . . that's something quite different from a governess. Beratoner's voice is getting louder. Beatrice quite clearly hears him say, 'You must be a regular idiot.' Ah, let them take you for an idiot, Fritz. Take it on the chin. What, don't you believe him, scoundrel? You're trying to tease his secret out of him? Can you guess? Has someone said something to you already? And again she hears Fritz whispering, but she can't make out the words. And there was Beratoner's voice again, deep and rough, 'What, a married woman? Come off it. Likely story.' Won't you shut up, scoundrel! She feels that she has never in her life hated anyone as much as this young boy who's slandering her without knowing she's the one he's slandering. What, Fritz? Louder, for goodness' sake! 'Left already.' What? I've left already? Oh, that's good, Fritz, you want to protect me from suspicion. She listens. She sucks in his words. 'A villa by the lake . . . Her husband's a lawyer.' No, what a swindler! How beautifully he lies. She could have been quite entertained if fear wasn't welling up within her. What? The husband's incredibly jealous? He's threatened to kill her if he ever caught her up to anything? What? By four o'clock this morning . . . Every night . . . Every . . .

night ... Enough, enough, enough! Won't you just be quiet? Have you no shame? Why are you sullying me like this? Even if your innocent friend doesn't know it's me you're talking about, you do. Why not just lie! That's enough! That's enough! And she really wants to block her ears, but instead she listens all the more intently. Not a syllable escapes her now, and in despair she hears from her sweet boy's lips the detailed description of the blissful nights he has spent in her arms, hears it in words that scream down on her like whiplashes, in expressions that she is hearing for the first time and yet which, rapidly understood, send hot shame pulsing to her brow. She knows that everything Fritz is saying outside in the garden is nothing but the truth, and yet at the same time she feels that that truth is already ceasing to be the truth – that this wretched chatter is reducing their bliss to filth and lies. And she had belonged to him. Given herself to him, the first since she was free. Her teeth chattered, her cheeks, her brow were burning, her knees rubbing themselves raw on the floor. Suddenly she gave a start. Rudi Beratoner wanted to see the house? And why had the people already left in the middle of the loveliest summer? 'But I don't believe a word of the whole story. A lawyer's wife? Ridiculous. Shall I tell you who it is?' She listens with her ears, with her heart, with all her senses. But not a word comes. Yet although she can't see she knows that Beratoner is indicating the house with his eyes; yes, the very window behind which she is kneeling. And now comes Fritz's answer. 'What are you thinking of? You're off your head.' And his companion: 'Don't say a word. I've only just realized. Congratulations. Not everyone has it as cosy as that. Yes, I know her. But if I wanted –' Beatrice didn't want to hear another word. Even she didn't know how she managed it. Perhaps it was the rushing of the blood in her brain that masked Beratoner's final words. For some time the talking outside was submerged in that rushing sound, before she could hear Fritz's words once again: 'Don't say a thing. She might be at home.' It's taken you long enough to think of that, my sweet boy. 'If only,' said Beratoner in a loud and impertinent voice. Then Fritz whispered again, quick and excited, and suddenly Beatrice heard the two of them rising from the bench outside. For heaven's sake, what's happening now? She threw herself lengthwise on the floor, so that she couldn't have been spotted through a crack from outside. Shadows seemed to slip past the shutters. Footsteps crunched over the gravel, a few muffled words were heard, then a quiet laugh, further away, and then nothing more. She waited. Nothing moved. Then she heard the voices again, further outside in the garden, echoing, and then nothing, nothing for a long time, until she was finally convinced that they had gone. They had probably climbed over the fence, just as they had come, and were still telling each other their stories outside. Was there anything left to say? Had Fritz left anything out? Well, he would be catching up now. And in that exquisite way of his he'll probably be making a few things up to impress Rudi Beratoner. Why not? Yes, that's the merry life of youth. One of them has his sister's governess, the other has his schoolmate's mother and the third a baroness who used to be an actress. Yes, the young gentlemen could all join in; they knew their women and could boldly assert that one was much like another.

And Beatrice whimpered silently to herself. She was still lying stretched out on the floor. What's the point of getting up right now? If she did decide to, it could only be with a view to putting an end to things. The idea of meeting Fritz and the other one again! She would have spat in their faces, struck them in the face with her fists. But would that not be a release, a pleasure – to hurl herself at them, scream in their faces: you boys, you scoundrels, aren't you ashamed, aren't you ashamed? . . . But at the same time she knows she won't do it. She feels it wouldn't even be worth the trouble, since she is determined, must be determined to take a path on which no slander and scorn can follow her. Never again, she can never, the fallen woman, appear in human society again. She has only one more thing to do on earth: to bid farewell to the only one who is dear to her – her son! To him alone. But of course without his noticing. Only she will know that she is leaving him for all eternity, that she is kissing her beloved child's brow for the last time. But how strange it was to think such things, stretched out on the floor, motionless. If someone were suddenly to walk into the room, he would certainly think she was dead. Where will they find me? she went on thinking. How will I accomplish it? How will I end up lying there insensibly, never again to awaken?

A sound in the hall made her tremble. Hugo had come home. She heard him outside, walking down the corridor past her door, open his own; and then there was silence again. He was back. She was no longer alone. Slowly, her limbs aching, she rose to her feet. It was almost completely dark in the room; and the air suddenly seemed unbearably oppressive to her. She didn't understand why she had actually lain for so long on the floor, and why she hadn't opened the shutters before. She hastily did so now, and the garden spread out before her, the mountains loomed, the sky darkened, and she felt as though she had seen none of it for many days and nights. The little world spread out in the evening so wonderfully peacefully that Beatrice grew more peaceful as well; but at the same time she felt an anxiety quietly rising within her, that this peace might be deceiving and confusing her. And she said to herself: what I have heard I have heard, what has happened has happened; the tranquillity of this evening, the peace of this world is nothing for me; a morning will come, the noise of the day will rise again, people will still be wicked and shoddy and love a dirty joke. And I'm someone who will never be able to forget it, not by day and not by night, not in loneliness and not when pleasure returns, not at home and not abroad. And I have nothing more to do in this world than to press a farewell kiss on my boy's beloved brow and go. What could he be doing now, alone in his room? From his open window a dull patch of light flowed over the gravel and the lawn. Was he lying in bed already – exhausted by the joys and exertions of his outing? A shudder ran through her body, a strange emotional combination of anxiety, of repulsion, of longing. Yes, she longed for him, but for someone other than the one lying there in his room bearing the scent of Fortunata's body on his own. She longed for the Hugo of times past, the fresh, pure boy who had once told him of the kiss of the little girl at dance class, the Hugo with whom she had driven through green valleys on a fine summer's day – and she wished for the time when she too had been someone else, a mother worthy of her son, rather than the sort of female that depraved boys could discuss in obscene language, as if talking about any old whore. Oh, if only there were such a thing as miracles! But there aren't. Never will she be able to erase that moment when, crouched on aching knees and with burning cheeks, she thirstily listened to the story of her disgrace – and her joy;

even in ten, twenty, fifty years, as a very old man, Rudi Beratoner will recall the hour when, as a young lad, he sat on a white bench in the garden of Frau Beatrice Heinold and a schoolmate told him how he lay in bed with her night after night until the grey dawn. She shook herself, she wrung her hands, she looked up to the sky, which met her lonely sorrow with silence and harboured no miracles. A dim confusion of sounds rose up to her from the lake and the road, the mountains reached towards the twinkling night sky, the yellow field glowed dully in the creeping gloom. How long did she intend to stay here motionless like this? What was she waiting for? Had she forgotten that Hugo, just as he had come, could vanish from the house again, to see someone who now meant more to him than she did? There was not much time to lose. She quickly unbolted her door, walked into the little drawing-room and stood by Hugo's door. She hesitated for a moment, listened, heard nothing and quickly opened the door.

Hugo sat on his divan staring wide-eyed at his mother as if startled from deep sleep. Flitting across his brow were strange shadows from the unsteady light of the electric lamp which, with its green shade, stood on the table in the middle of the room. Beatrice stopped by the door for a while. Hugo threw his head back, looking as though he were about to rise to his feet; but he sat where he was, his arms stretched away from his sides, his hands propped on the couch. Beatrice felt the paralysis of the moment with heart-rending pain. An unparalleled fear seized her soul, and she said to herself: he knows everything. What's going to happen? she thought in the same breath. She walked over to him, forced a cheerful expression and asked, 'Have you slept, Hugo?' 'No, mother,' he answered, 'I just lay down for a while.' She looked into a pale, tormented child's face: an unspeakable sympathy, in which her own misery was submerged, welled up in her, she laid her fingers on his tousled hair, still shyly, wrapped her arms around his head, sat down beside him and tenderly began 'Well, my boy' – yet she couldn't think of what to say next. His features twisted violently; she took his hands in hers, he pressed them distractedly, stroked her fingers, cast his eyes sideways, his smile grew mask-like, his eyes reddened, his chest began to rise and fall, all of a sudden he slid from the divan, lay at his mother's feet with his head in her lap and wept bitterly. Beatrice, deeply shaken and yet quite liberated, since she felt that he was not estranged from her, said nothing at first, let him weep, gently buried her fingers in his hair and wondered, mortally afraid: what can have happened? And immediately consoled herself: maybe nothing in particular. Perhaps only that his nerves were failing. And she remembered her husband being susceptible to very similar convulsive attacks, for no apparent reason; after the excitement of some great role or another, after some kind of experience that had wounded his actor's vanity, or apparently without any reason at all, or at least none that she was able to discover. And all of a sudden the question welled up in her, whether Ferdinand had not sometimes wept over disappointments and torments which he might have found tolerable if he had been married to someone else? But why should she worry about that! Whatever crimes he had committed, he had paid for them, and it was all so long, so long ago. Now her son was the one weeping in her lap, and she knew that he was doing it for Fortunata's sake. What sorrow the sight of it caused her. What depths swallowed up her own experience, faced as she was now with her son's emotional torment. Where were her disgrace and torment and mortal longing disappearing to, faced with the burning desire to give heart into the creature weeping in her lap. And in the overwhelming urge to make him feel better, she whispered, 'Don't cry, my boy. Everything will be all right again.' And as he began to shake his head, 'No', in her lap, she repeated more resolutely, 'Everything will be fine again, believe me.' And she realized that she was addressing the phrase not only to Hugo but to herself as well. If it was within her power to help her son back out of his despair, to fire him with new courage to face life, then it was only because she was aware that it was his gratitude, the fact of his belonging to her once more, that gave her the chance, the duty and the strength to go on living. And all of a sudden the picture of that imaginary landscape rose up in her, the one where she had once dreamed of strolling with him; and promisingly, at the same time, the idea came to her: what if I set off, with Hugo, on the journey I had planned before that terrible moment came upon me? And what if we never returned from that journey? And what if, away, abroad, far from all the people we have known, where the air is pure, we began a new and a finer life?

Then he suddenly raised his head from her lap, with confused eyes and twisted lips, and hoarsely cried, 'No, no, it won't be all right.' And rose to his feet, looked vacantly at his mother, took a few steps towards the table as if looking for something there, walked back and forth in the room a few times with his head bowed, and finally stopped motionlessly at the window, his gaze turned towards the darkness. 'Hugo,' called his mother, who had been following him with her eyes, but who didn't feel capable of rising from the couch. And once again, pleadingly, 'Hugo, my boy!' Then he turned towards her, again with that fixed smile that now caused her more pain than his outburst. And, trembling, she asked again, 'What's happened?'

'Nothing, mother,' he answered with a kind of rapt serenity.

Now she rose resolutely to her feet and walked over to him. 'Do you know why I came into your room?' He just looked at her. 'Go on, guess.' He shook his head. 'I wanted to ask if you'd like to take a little trip with me. 'A trip,' he repeated, apparently uncomprehending. 'Yes, Hugo, a trip – to Italy. We have time, school doesn't start for three weeks. We could be back ages before then. So, what do you think?' 'I don't know,' he answered. She put her arm around his neck. How like Ferdinand he looks, she thought suddenly. Once he played the part of a very young fellow, and he looked exactly like that. And she joked: 'So, if you don't know, Hugo, then I know very definitely that we're going to go on our travels. Yes, my boy, there's nothing more to be said on the subject. And now, dry your eyes, cool your brow and we'll set off together.' 'Set off?' 'Yes, why not? It's Sunday and there's nothing to eat in the house. And we have a date with the others down in the hotel. And the moonlit outing across the lake! Didn't you know that was supposed to be happening tonight?' 'Wouldn't you rather go on your own, mother? I could follow you later.' She was suddenly seized by a deranged anxiety. Did he want her to go away? Why? For heaven's sake! She suppressed the terrible thought. And, mustering her self-control, she said, 'Aren't you hungry yet?' 'No,' he replied. 'I'm not either, really. Why don't we go for a walk first?' 'A walk?' 'Yes, and then let's take a little detour to the Lake Hotel.' He hesitated for a moment.

She stood there, tense and waiting. Finally he nodded. 'Fine, mother. Go and get yourself ready.' 'Oh, I am ready, I'll just have to put my coat on.' She didn't stir from the spot. He didn't seem to notice, walked to his washbasin, poured water into his hand from the jug and cooled his brow, eyes and cheeks. Then he quickly ran his comb through his hair a few times. 'Yes, just tidy yourself up,' said Beatrice. And she had the oppressive sense that she had often said those words to Ferdinand in times long past as he was preparing to go out . . . God knows where to. Hugo picked up his hat and said with a smile, 'I'm ready, mother.' Now she dashed to her bedroom, fetched her coat and only buttoned it when she was back in the room with Hugo, who had been quietly waiting for her. 'Come on, then,' she said.

As the two of them left the house, the maid returned from her Sunday walk. Despite the subservience of her greeting, all of a sudden Beatrice understood, from an almost imperceptible lowering of the maid's eyes, that she knew everything that had gone on in the house over the past few weeks. – But she didn't greatly care. Now she was indifferent to everything apart from the feeling of happiness, the happiness she had missed for so long, at having Hugo by her side.

They continued through the meadows beneath the silent night-blue of the sky, walking close together, as quickly as though they had a destination in mind. At first they didn't say a word. But before they stepped into the darkness of the wood, Beatrice turned to her son: 'Won't you link arms with me, Hugo?' He took her arm, and she felt better. They went on walking in the heavy shade of the trees, their dense network of branches penetrated here and there by a light from one of the villas deep in the valley. Beatrice slipped her hand over Hugo's, stroked it, then raised it to her lips and kissed it. He put up no resistance. No, he knew nothing about her. Or was he just putting up with it? Did he understand, even though she was his mother? Soon they passed through a broad, greenish-blue strip of light that fell in front of the park gate of the Welponers' villa. Now they could have seen one another face to face, but they went on gazing ahead into the dark that immediately swallowed them both. In this part of the wood the darkness was so dense that they had to slow down their steps to avoid stumbling. 'Be careful,' Beatrice said from time to time. Hugo shook his head, and they clung tighter to one another. After a while there was a path which, as they knew from the daylight hours, led down to the lake. They turned off into the path and soon stepped back into a dull brightness where the trees, further apart, opened into a meadow clearing, with the sky still starless above. Worn wooden steps led from here, with an unsteady rail for support, down to the country road that lost itself in the night, on the right-hand side; but, on the left, these led back to the town, from which countless stars shimmered. In silent accord, Beatrice and Hugo turned in this direction. And as if their walk together through the darkness made her more intimate with him without any need for words, Beatrice said, in an innocuous, almost jocular tone, 'Hugo, I don't like it when you cry.' He didn't reply, looking deliberately away from her over the steel-grey lake, which now stretched in a narrow strip along the mountains above. 'Once upon a time,' Beatrice began again, a sigh in her voice, 'once, you told me everything.' And, as she said it, she felt all of a sudden as though she were really addressing her words to Ferdinand, and as though she wanted to extract from her dead husband all the secrets that he had disdainfully kept from her while he was still alive. Am I going mad? she thought, am I mad already? And as though to recall herself to reality she gripped Hugo's arm so tightly that he twitched, almost in fear. But she went on talking: 'Mightn't it be easier for you, Hugo, if you told me?' And she linked arms with him again. But while her own question resonated within her, she silently felt that she had not asked the question out of any desire to relieve Hugo's soul, but that she was also falling prey to a strange kind of curiosity, of which she felt profoundly ashamed. And Hugo, as if sensing the mysterious vagueness of her question, didn't answer, and let his arm slide from hers as though unintentionally. Disappointed and alone, Beatrice went on walking beside him along the sad road. What am I in the world, she wondered anxiously, if I am not his mother? Is today the day when I must lose everything? Am I nothing more than the name of a sloven in the mouths of corrupt young boys? And that feeling of togetherness with Hugo, of shared security up in the sweet darkness of the forest, was all of that merely illusion? Then life is no longer to be borne, then everything is really over. But why does the idea frighten me so? Was it not resolved long ago? Had I not already decided to put an end to everything? And didn't I know that there was nothing left for me? And behind her, creeping after her in the darkness of the road there hissed, like mocking ghosts, the terrible words that she had first heard through the crack in the window, the words which meant her love and her shame, her bliss and her death. And as though thinking of a sister she thought for a moment of that other girl who had once run along a beach, tormented by evil spirits, exhausted with pleasure and anguish . . .

They were approaching the village. The light that fell broadly across the water a few hundred paces away came from the terrace where her friends were dining and waiting for her. To step again into such a shaft of life seemed insane to Beatrice, completely beyond the realms of possibility. Why did she take that path? Why did she stay at Hugo's side? How cowardly to want to say goodbye to the one to whom she was nothing more than an irritating woman trying to invade his secrets. Then, suddenly, she saw his eyes turned upon her again with a beseeching expression that awoke new fear and hope within her. 'Hugo,' she said. And he said, belatedly replying to a question that she had already forgotten, 'It can't be all right again. There's nothing to be said. It just can't.' 'But Hugo,' she cried as though relieved that he had broken the silence, 'of course it will be all right, we'll go away, Hugo, far away.' 'What good will that do us, mother?' Us –? That goes for me too! But isn't it better that way? Doesn't it bring us closer together? He was walking more quickly, she was keeping up with him, when suddenly he stopped, looked out over the lake and breathed in deeply as though comfort and peace were coming to him from the loneliness over the water. Out there a few illuminated boats were drifting along. Could that be our party? Beatrice thought fleetingly. They won't have any moonlight. And suddenly she had an idea. 'What would you say, Hugo,' she said, 'to the two of us going out there . . . alone?' He gazed up to the sky as though looking for the moon. Beatrice understood and said, 'We don't need it.' 'What will we do out there on the dark water?' he asked faintly. She grasped his head, looked into his eyes and said, 'You can tell me. You can tell me what's happened to you, as you always used to.' She guessed that out there,

89

in the dark loneliness of that familiar lake, he would shake off the shyness that kept him from telling his mother what had happened. Sensing no further resistance in his silence, she turned resolutely towards the boathouse where her little boat was stored. The wooden door was ajar. She and Hugo walked into the dark room, unchained the boat as if the moment were not to be lost, and then she swung herself into it, Hugo following her. He took one of the oars, pushed off, and an instant later the open sky was above them. Hugo took the other oar, and guided the boat along the shore and past the Lake Hotel, so close that that they could hear the voices from the terrace. Beatrice thought she could hear the architect's voice above the others. The individual forms and faces were indistinguishable. How easy it was to get away from people! Right now what do I care, thought Beatrice, what they say, think or know about me? You just push a boat away from the shore and drift so closely past people that you can hear their voices, and yet nothing matters! If you don't come back . . . the words echoed more deeply within her, and she trembled slightly. – She sat by the rudder and guided the boat towards the middle of the lake. Still the moon had not risen, but the water all around, as though it had stored the daytime sun within it, surrounded the boat in a dull circle of light. From time to time a shaft of light came from the shore, and in it Beatrice thought she could see Hugo's face becoming fresher and more carefree. When they were quite far out, Hugo lowered the oars, removed his coat and opened his shirt collar. How like his father he is, thought Beatrice with painful surprise. Only I never knew him as young as this. And how handsome he is. His features are nobler than Ferdinand's. But I never knew them, or his voice either, they were always other people's voices and faces. Am I seeing him for the first time now? . . . And a deep shudder ran through her. But now that the boat was entirely in the night-black shadow of the mountains, Hugo's features began to blur. He started rowing again, but very slowly, and they hardly moved from the spot. Now would be the right time, thought Beatrice, but for a moment she had no idea what it was time for, until all of a sudden, as if she were waking from a dream, the desire to know what Hugo had been through burned its way through her senses. And she asked, 'So, Hugo, what happened?' He only shook his head. But she, with mounting excitement, felt that his refusal was no longer serious. 'Do say something, Hugo,' she said. 'You can tell me anything. I know so much already. You can imagine.' And as if trying to exorcize one last spell, she whispered the name into the night: 'Fortunata'.

A shudder passed through Hugo's body, so violent that it seemed to transmit itself on to the boat. Beatrice continued her question: 'You were with her today – and this is how you come home? What has she done to you, Hugo?' Hugo said nothing, went on evenly rowing, looked into the air. Suddenly it came to Beatrice like an epiphany. She pressed her hand to her brow as though she couldn't understand why she hadn't guessed before, and, leaning close to Hugo, she quickly whispered, 'The captain from over the sea was there, wasn't he? And he found you with her?' Hugo looked up. 'The captain?'

Only now did it occur to her that the man she meant wasn't a captain at all. 'I mean the Baron,' she said. 'He was there? He found the two of you? He insulted you? He beat you, Hugo?'

'No, mother, the man you're speaking of wasn't there. I don't know him. I swear to you, mother.'

'What, then?' asked Beatrice. 'She doesn't love you any more? She's had enough of you? She's spurned you? Shown you the door? Is that it, Hugo?'

'No, mother.' And he fell silent.

'So, Hugo, what is it? Tell me.'

'Don't ask, mother, don't ask. It's too dreadful.'

Now the flames of her curiosity flickered to life. She felt that the day's confusion, so filled with mysteries, old and new, must finally yield an answer from somewhere or other. She clutched at the air with both hands as though to grasp something fluttering by. She slipped down from the tiller and sat at Hugo's feet. 'Tell me, then,' she began, 'you can tell me everything, you don't have to be shy, I understand everything! Everything. I'm your mother, Hugo, and I'm a woman. Bear that in mind, I'm a woman as well. You mustn't fear that you could hurt me, that you could wound my tender feelings. I've been through a lot recently. I'm not yet an . . . old woman. I understand everything. Too much, my son . . . You mustn't think that we are so far apart, Hugo, and that there are things you mustn't say to me.' She felt with confused astonishment how much she was exposing herself, how tempting she was. 'Oh, if you knew, Hugo, if you only knew.' And the answer came: 'I know, mother.' Beatrice trembled. But she no longer felt any shame, only a liberating awareness of being closer to him, of belonging to him. She sat at his feet on the floor of the boat and took his hands in hers. 'Tell me,' she whispered.

And he spoke, but he told her nothing. With dull and fragmented words he only explained that he could never again show himself in human company. What had happened to him today banished him for ever from the realm of the living.

'What, what has happened?'

'I wasn't quite myself. – I don't know what happened. They got me drunk.'

'They got you drunk? Who, who? – You were – you weren't alone with Fortunata?' It occurred to her that she had recently seen him in the company of Wilhelmine Fallehn and the circus rider. So it was them? And, gasping, she asked again, 'What's happened?' But without Hugo saying anything she already knew. A picture painted itself before her eyes in the night, and while she tried to turn her eyes from it in horror it followed her with shameless impertinence beneath her closed lids. And, with a new and terrible realization, opening her eyes again and focusing them rigidly on Hugo's mutely pressed lips, invisible to her, she asked, 'You've known since today? They told you?'

He didn't reply, but a convulsion passed through his whole body, so wildly that it hurled him submissively on to the floor of the boat by Beatrice's side. She merely groaned once, in despair, and in a shudder of unutterable abandon once more grasped Hugo's feverishly trembling hands which had slipped from hers. This time he let her hold them, and that made her feel better. She drew him closer to her, pressing herself to him; a painful longing rose from the depths of her soul and spilled darkly into his. And they both felt as if their boat, although it was almost motionless, was moving further and further, at ever increasing speed. Where was it taking her? Through what goalless dream? Towards what lawless world? Must he ever return to dry land? Could he ever? They were united on the same journey, the sky in its clouds held no new dawn for them; and in the seductive anticipation of eternal night they abandoned their lips to one another.

The boat drifted onwards, towards the most distant shore, and Beatrice felt as though in that moment, for the first time she was kissing someone she had never known, someone who had been her husband.

When she felt herself returning to consciousness, she mustered the emotional strength required to keep her from fully waking up. Clutching both of Hugo's hands in her own, she swung herself on to the edge of the boat. When the boat tilted to the side, Hugo's eyes opened, and in his face a glimmer of fear sought for one last time to unite him with the common lot of humanity. Beatrice drew to her breast her beloved, her son, the boy destined for death. Understanding, forgiving, redeemed, he closed his eyes; but her own eyes saw the rising grey shore in the menacing gloom, and before the tepid waves pushed between her lids, her dying gaze drank in the final shadow of the fading world.